D0090465

THE
December Rose

Also by
Leon Garfield

THE GHOST DOWNSTAIRS
GUILT AND GINGERBREAD
JACK HOLBORN
JOHN DIAMOND
MISTER CORBETT'S GHOST

Leon Garfield

THE *December Rose*

VIKING KESTREL

To

Paul and Renny

VIKING KESTREL
Penguin Books Ltd, Harmondsworth, Middlesex, England
Viking Penguin Inc., 40 West 23rd Street, New York, New York 10010, U.S.A.
Penguin Books Australia Ltd, Ringwood, Victoria, Australia
Penguin Books Canada Limited, 2801 John Street, Markham, Ontario, Canada L3R 1B4
Penguin Books (N.Z.) Ltd, 182–190 Wairau Road, Auckland 10, New Zealand

First published 1986
Published simultaneously in paperback by Puffin Books
Reprinted 1987

Based on the BBC TV production

Filmset in Monophoto Photina
Printed in Great Britain by
Richard Clay Ltd, Bungay, Suffolk

British Library Cataloguing in Publication Data available
ISBN 0-670-81054-1

Library of Congress Catalog Card Number:
86-40576

ONE

At about a quarter past five on a Thursday afternoon early in September, a woman entered the Post Office at Charing Cross and inquired of one of the clerks if a letter was awaiting her. It was her third visit in as many days. On this occasion the clerk was able to oblige her. He handed her a letter which she opened immediately, without even stepping back from the counter. She glanced rapidly to see the name of the sender, as if to reassure herself, and then, clutching the letter in her hand, hastened outside with an air of strong nervous excitement.

Although the day was warm and summery, she was dressed entirely in black . . . which served to set off the extreme pallor of her complexion and the brilliancy of her eyes. Her name was Donia Vassilova. She was known as an enemy of the country and a grave risk to the security of the State.

Once outside, she hesitated briefly, glanced about her, and then set off in the direction of Charing Cross Road. She walked quickly, sometimes stepping out into the road rather than be restricted to the slower pace of those ahead of her.

From time to time she paused, looked behind her, and then hastened on. It was plain that she suspected she was being followed, but could not be sure who, among the shifting multitude behind her, was her pursuer.

She turned into Moor Street and then into Greek Street, where she stopped abruptly and gazed up searchingly at one of the houses on the right-hand side. Possibly she did this with the intention of deceiving her pursuer, or perhaps she hoped she would be seen by a confederate and her predicament understood.

After a few moments, during which she showed signs of agitation, she hurried northward into Oxford Street where she attempted to lose herself by mingling with the dense crowds. However, her striking appearance always rendered her an easy object for observation. Becoming aware of this, she sought out the less frequented streets to the north, doubtless hoping to isolate her pursuer and force him to show himself. On one occasion she stood for a full five minutes on a corner, intently staring back along the way she had come. Although she saw nothing to confirm her suspicion, she was by no means satisfied and continued with her evasive antics of hurrying from street to street, now north, now east, now south . . .

At half past eight, the evening, which had been increasing in heaviness, turned very dark and came on to rain. The woman, after sheltering briefly in a doorway, went into the Adam and Eve public house in the Tottenham Court Road, where she occupied a seat by the window from which she could observe the street outside. Then, for the first time since she had collected it from the Post Office, she read the letter. As she did so, it could be seen that her hand went continually to a trinket that she wore on a chain round her neck. It was a gold locket bearing an unusual design in black enamel: an eagle . . .

The rain persisted for just over an hour, during which time the woman remained in her place by the window, dividing her attention between her letter and the street, and speaking to no one apart from the waiter who served her. She left the public house at a quarter to ten, crossed the Tottenham Court Road, and walked in the direction of the City.

She seemed to have abandoned her earlier attempts at evasion. She no longer hesitated, but walked rapidly and with a definite sense of purpose. Perhaps she thought she had thrown off her pursuer – either that, or the need to meet with her confederates and inform them of the letter had become too urgent to admit of further delay. The only time she paused was in Fetter Lane, and then only briefly.

She looked behind her. She saw no one. The rain had emptied all the streets, and the lamps, shining on the wet, made watchers only of shadows. The pallor of her face was extraordinary; her eyes were enormous. It was possible that among the multitude of shadows that inhabited the doorways, one had suddenly seemed darker and more threatening than was natural. She drew in her breath and, with a violent shake of her head, hurried away towards Blackfriars.

She reached Bridge Street and then, after a moment's indecision, decided that, rather than crossing the bridge, her best course lay among the narrow lanes and alleys off Union Street. For a little while she negotiated them with the skill and cunning of an animal until, suddenly, in Stonecutter Alley, a deep puddle obstructed her way. Instinctively she shrank back, as if more careful for her skirts than for her life. Such folly!

She turned aside into Pilgrim Court. Even as she did so, she realized her mistake. Pilgrim Court was a dead end. There was no way out. Just before she vanished into the darkness, she turned, and her face was caught in the dim yellow of a street lamp. The expression on it was one that would have been better unseen. It was a look of terror, hatred and despair; and the hatred was the strongest and the worst.

She made no great struggle and uttered only the faintest of cries. All her strength and determination were directed towards clutching the locket. Indeed, her grip upon it remained so strong that it required considerable force to prise it from her hand before her body was tipped into the river off Blackfriars Stairs. She floated briefly, with her face upwards, before the stone that was attached to her waist by a rope dragged her down.

The chain on the locket had been broken, but otherwise it was quite undamaged: '. . . as you can see for yourself, m'lord.'

TWO

There was a boy up the chimney, but only God and Mister Roberts knew exactly where. How God came by His knowledge was, of course, a holy mystery; and how Mister Roberts came by his was almost as wonderful an affair. He'd only to lay his ear against a wall, medically so to speak, as if it was a wheezy chest, and it was enough! Leaving a black ear behind, he'd rush to the nearest fireplace, insert his head, and bellow upwards: 'I knows yer, Barnacle! I knows ye're just squattin' up there, a-pickin' of yer nose! Git on with yer sweepin', lad, or I'll light a fire and scorch yer to a black little twig! So help me,' he would add, for he was a devout man, 'God!'

Up and up the dreadful threat would fly, booming and echoing through all the narrow, dark and twisty flues, until it found out Barnacle, exactly as Mister Roberts had divined, squatting in some sooty nook and, if there was room enough to move his arms, a-picking of his nose.

'I knows yer – yer – yer – yer . . . Git on – on – on – on . . . scorch yer – yer – yer – yer . . .'

Barnacle, neatly wedged in an elbow of broken brick, went on with picking his nose and waiting for 'God!'.

His proper name was Absalom Brown, but his owner, Mister Roberts, called him Barnacle on account of his amazing powers of holding on. He could attach himself to the inside of a flue by finger- and toe-holds at which even a fly might have blinked. It was a real gift, and the only one he had. Otherwise he was a child of darkness, no better, as Mister Roberts often had cause to shout, than a animal.

'So help me, God – God – God – God!' came Mister Roberts's voice, and Barnacle began brushing away at the soot, and dislodged a piece of brickwork for good measure. He heard it go bumping and rattling down until at last it clanged to a stop against the iron bars of a distant grate.

'Watch it, lad – lad – lad – lad!'

'Watch it, 'e says,' marvelled Barnacle, who was as tight in blackness as a stone in a plum. 'An' wot wiv, might I arst?'

Eyes weren't any help, as it was as dark outside his head as it was within; and anyway he was too bone-idle to open them. It was fingers, elbows and knees that told him where he was, and it was his nose that told him where he was going, and, most important of all, it was his ears that warned him of what was to come: either the wrath of Mister Roberts or a sudden fall of stinking, choking soot that was always heralded by a tiny whispering click.

Cautiously he eased himself up the flue, clearing the soot as he went, partly with his brush and partly with the spiky stubble that grew out of his head. Once he'd had a cap, but he'd lost it in his infancy, trying to swipe at a pigeon as he'd come out of the top of a chimney-pot. He'd cried bitterly over the loss, not of the cap but of the handsome brass badge on the front of it that had proclaimed him to be a boy of importance, a climbing boy belonging to a master sweep.

Presently he found he could move more easily. Either he was shrinking or the flue was getting wider. He paused and sniffed. There was a new smell. Mingled in with the sulphurous stink of soot was a faint aroma of toast. He divined he was approaching a coming together of God knew how many flues rising up from God knew how many fireplaces, for the house he was crawling about in, like an earwig, was a real monster, big as Parliament, almost.

He went on a little further and tried the darkness again. To his great pleasure he found he could move his arms enough to pick his nose. He sighed and reclined luxuriously against a thick cushion of soot. For a few brief moments he was happy, being no more than a sensation in the dark.

He could hear voices. They were very faint, scarcely more than murmurs, drifting up from somewhere far below. He listened. He liked listening. In fact, it was his only schooling, and his lessons were made up out of whispers, quarrels, sly kisses, laughter and tears.

There were several voices and, little by little, he began to make them out. There was one that was smooth and thin, like a bone, and another that was a real wobbling fat-guts of a voice. There was a lady who laughed whenever she said anything, and there was a fourth voice that was hard to put a shape to. It was a voice with a kind of whistling edge to it, which seemed to cut through the quiet without even making it bleed.

'. . . as you can see for yourself, m'lord,' said Whistling Edge.

'Why, it's charming, charming,' twittered Laughing Lady. 'And so unusual, don't you think?'

'Well done,' wobbled Fat-Guts. 'Well done indeed!'

'A sorry business, but villains must pay the price,' murmured Smooth-and-Bony. 'We owe you much!'

'The *December Rose*,' said Whistling Edge. 'We will be waiting.'

'The *December Rose*!' repeated Fat-Guts, and Smooth-and-Bony echoed him, 'The *December Rose*!', while Laughing Lady chuckled, like pebbles in the rain.

Eagerly Barnacle poked a finger in his ear and reamed out the soot. He wanted to hear more. He leaned forward, perilously. Suddenly he felt something thin and cold creep up the side of his leg. A moment later he felt a sharp, stabbing pain, as if he'd been stung by a chimney snake!

It was Mister Roberts. Suspecting that his boy was idling, he'd shoved his sweeping rods up the chimney with a spike on the end of them instead of his brush. It was his own invention. 'Nothin' like it,' he'd declare, 'for unstopperin' even the tightest lad!'

He was right. Barnacle howled – and jerked. He crashed his head, scraped his back and skinned his elbows and knees. Frantically he clutched at the blackness, kicked at the air, and howled again. He was falling. Despairingly he clawed at the rushing brickwork, but his amazing powers had deserted him, and he left only fingertips behind.

His rush down to hell – for that's where he was going and no mistake: everybody had always told him so – was tremendous, and accompanied by a furious storm of soot and rubble.

'Gawd 'elp us!' he shrieked, and awaited the iron fist of Grandmother Death.

A moment later, it came. His bones seemed to shoot out of their sockets and his teeth snapped together over the top of his head as, with immense force, he struck the bars of a grate. Then, with a contemptuous shrug of iron and brass, he was tossed out into a carpeted darkness that smelled of cigars and toast.

'What is it? What is it?'

'It's a nest –'

'It's an animal –'

'No, it's a boy,' said Whistling Edge.

He was not in hell. Mister Roberts's spike had jerked him and tipped him down another flue. He was in the room of voices.

'Yes . . . a climbing boy . . . a sweep's boy . . . only a boy –'

He opened his eyes. Instantly light blazed and half-blinded him. The room was huge and gleaming, with a crusty ceiling, like a cake . . .

'Come to me, boy,' said Whistling Edge, a dark and terrible figure, shaped like a coffin, with enormous square-toed boots.

'That's right, go to Inspector Creaker, boy,' urged Smooth-and-Bony. 'He won't hurt you.'

Whistling Edge smiled a smile of a thousand teeth. Barnacle, dazed and terrified, dragged himself upright, clutching at the fire-irons for support.

'Put that down, boy!'

He'd got hold of a poker. Whistling Edge took a pace back, Laughing Lady screamed, and the room was full of glaring, frightened eyes.

'Oh my Gawd – oh my Gawd!' came a familiar voice, as the door opened and round it came the sooty head of Mister Roberts, with his hair bolt upright and shame and horror all over his face. 'What the 'ell are you doin' in 'ere, lad? Beggin' yer honours' pardons! Come 'ere, you little turd! Drop that bleedin' poker or I'll kill yer, so 'elp me God, I will!'

He meant it; he always did. Barnacle screeched defiance and threw the poker at him. Something smashed, but it couldn't have been Mister Roberts, as he was able to shout, 'Like a animal! Just like a animal, 'e is!'

Whistling Edge – Inspector Creaker – began to advance. Barnacle's terror increased until it filled him from frowsy top to stinking toe. He had a natural horror of policemen, and this one was the worst he'd ever seen. He threw the tongs at him; and then, without any thought of the consequences, and feeling only a desperate longing to be elsewhere, to escape, to dart into some dark hole, he began to throw everything he could lay his hands on.

Vases, dishes, ornaments, cups and plates, jugs, a silver teapot and a china bust of the queen flew through the air as if of their own accord, and crashed and banged against walls and furnishings while the little black figure of Barnacle hopped and darted hither and thither, frantically seeking a way out.

'Stop him! Stop him!' shouted Fat-Guts. 'Stop him!' screamed Laughing Lady, shaking in a corner and blazing with beads. 'I'll kill yer!' panted Mister Roberts. But Whistling Edge was the worst. He seemed to know Barnacle's every twist and turn. There was no escaping him. His eyes bulged like cobble-stones, and his great square hands came nearer and nearer . . .

'Come to me, boy, come to me . . .'

'I'm a goner!' thought Barnacle, desperately clawing across a table for something more to throw. 'I'd 'ave been better orf in 'ell!'

He clutched a fistful of spoons and something glittering on a chain. He raised his fist, but even as he did so he knew that what he held was pitiful against a man like Whistling Edge.

'Come –' began the policeman, and then he stopped. He was staring at Barnacle's fist or, rather, at what was held in it. A strange look had come into his face, a look of infinite distress. He grew pale, as if his blood had turned to water and his flesh to stone.

For maybe two seconds – no more – he seemed unable to move. But two seconds were enough! With a scream of joy Barnacle darted under his outstretched arm, rushed across the room and hurled himself at the drawn curtains. Wood snapped, glass exploded and Barnacle, speckled with splinters, billowed through yellow velvet and out into the late afternoon!

He landed on grass, but only for an instant. No sooner had he touched it than he was off, like a black cinder whirled away by the wind. He ran and ran through streets and alleys and courts and squares, up hills, down steps, through markets and across wide thoroughfares thick with traffic. He ran until he could run no more. Gasping and panting, he leaned inside a doorway, trying to get back his breath. It was only then that he realized that there was still something clutched in his fist.

Cautiously he examined his prize. He frowned, and then he beamed. He was now the possessor of six silver teaspoons and a locket on a broken chain. It was a gold locket with a curiously enamelled design: a bird, an eagle, black as the hand that held it.

THREE

Property changes a man. It elevates him above the animals. Barnacle, deep in his dirty doorway, gazed down upon the mingled brightness that lay within his black fist, and a grimy little candle was kindled in his soul. For the very first time in his life he began to have thoughts that reached beyond the living instant that had always enveloped him like another skin. Wonderingly he contemplated the prospect of a Barnacle improved, a comfortable Barnacle, owning, among other things, a smaller, more ignorant Barnacle, who would fetch his food and beer. He beamed.

Such was the mysterious power of a golden locket and six silver spoons. Curiously he examined the locket. To his alarm, it seemed to come apart; then he was relieved to discover that it was only opening on a hinge. He whistled. Inside was a tiny painted picture of a lady with a baby in her arms.

He peered at it closely, for it was nearly evening and the light was fading fast. He sighed. The colours pleased him, but it was more than that. It was the faces. Although their eyes were no bigger than pinpricks and their smiling lips no more than scarlet specks, they gave off a powerful sweetness that turned the light inside him rosy and warm.

He shut the locket. He would keep it. He could get rich enough just from the spoons. Suddenly he scowled. He'd heard something that had alarmed him. Among the grinding noises of the town, he heard the voices of children, shouting and chanting:

'Eaver, Weaver, chimney-sweeper,
Had a wife and couldn't keep her –'

They'd spied a walking sweep. He poked his head out of the doorway and looked both ways. He was in a narrow alley inhabited only by fly-blown rubbish and clustering shadows. Nothing else. Cautiously he advanced –

'Took another, didn't love her –'

The unseen children were coming nearer; already he could make out the pelting rattle of running feet. Then the voices rose to a venomous screech:

'UP A CHIMNEY HE DID SHOVE HER!'

and round the corner came the object of their mockery. It was Mister Roberts, wobbling and hobbling and red-faced with rage!

'Barnacle!' howled the master sweep, forgetting his tormentors in the excitement of catching sight of his bolting boy. 'I'll kill yer!'

Barnacle vanished. In an instant he was gone from the alley, leaving no more than a shriek of dismay and a whiff of panic behind. He was out in the street, scuttling among hurrying feet and rolling wheels and lifted sticks and angry, jerking skirts.

Just how Mister Roberts had found him out was a deep and horrible mystery; but then most things were a mystery to Barnacle, so he wasn't surprised. He scampered round a corner, then another, and another, going off like a firecracker each time . . .

'Eaver, Weaver, chimney-sweeper,
Had a wife and couldn't keep her –'

The children were after *him*! He knew it. It was only natural. See a running boy and you've got to run after him. He'd have done it himself –

'Took another, didn't love her –'

Didn't love *him* either! Their voices came flying after him like arrows. He twisted again, sharp as a wish-bone. He screamed. He'd wished wrong! Straight ahead was a dirty great wall, all prickly with broken glass. He was in a dead end. He turned to go back, but it was too late!

'Up a chimney he did shove her!'

There they were, coming towards him! The lousy stinking children, all fists and boots and shrieks! From somewhere at the back he could hear Mister Roberts, screeching his insides out: 'Catch 'im! Catch 'im! A shillin' if yer gets 'im, dead or alive!'

He glared about him for something to throw: anything – a stone, a brick, a lump of wood. Frantically he tried to claw up a cobble; then, with a despairing scream of defiance, he hurled the only weapon he had. A fistful of silver spoons!

If, as he'd thrown the spoons, he'd prayed to God to save him, he'd have been a religious person for the rest of his life, for the yelling, shrieking monster of a hundred fists and feet stopped in its tracks. It swayed and tottered like smoke in the wind. Then, with little howls of 'Silver! Silver!', it turned into a struggling heap of children, biting and scratching for possession of the spoons.

Barnacle fled. Nobody wanted him any more. He wasn't worth as much as spoons. He scuttled away at a tremendous rate, and Mister Roberts, cursing the greed of his helpers, limped and panted after his bolting boy.

Barnacle's chimney nature led him among the dark and narrow ways behind the main thoroughfare. Solitary street lamps, posted on corners like burning policemen, glared down mistily, now catching him, now losing him, in a prison of yellow light.

He was weary and aching but a million miles from despair. He still owned property. Though he'd flung away most of his fortune, he had something left. Clutched in his fist, so fiercely that they bit into his flesh, were the locket and a single silver spoon. He was prepared to keep on running to the end of the world.

But though his spirit was willing, his breath was getting ragged and his twiggy black legs were beginning to fail. His soul might have carried on, but the rest of him was almost done for. Gasping and groaning with effort, he pelted down a last street, whirled blindly round a last corner and thumped, with sickening force, straight into a brick wall!

'Oi!' grunted the wall, staggering under the unexpected blow. 'Watch where you're goin', lad! You caught me fair and square in the supper!'

The wall had sprouted an enormous pair of arms, and Barnacle found himself seized in a grip there was no escaping.

'Lemme go! Lemme go!' he wailed, struggling pitifully. ''E'll kill me!'

'Oh?' inquired the wall, weirdly turning itself into a giant of a man with a huge puzzled face. 'And who's going to kill you, lad?'

For answer, Barnacle twisted his head until it nearly came off at the neck and did what he always did. He bit the arm that was gripping him.

'Ow! You little savage!' cried the man, for Barnacle's teeth were as sharp as a puppy's, and they'd drawn blood. 'I'll –' he began, lifting a hand as big as a shovel, when, from half a street away, came a hoarse and horrible voice:

'Barnacle! Barnacle, yer little turd! I'll kill yer . . . so 'elp me, I will!'

For an instant, the man hesitated; then, opening the door of the public house from which he'd just emerged, he tipped Barnacle inside. 'Wait in there!' he muttered, and shut the door.

Barnacle collapsed. He sniffed. The air was as thick as a stew. It stank of beer, onions and tobacco. All around him there was a creaking and grunting of high-backed pews as their inhabitants turned to see what the night had blown in. Barnacle shrank into himself, which, all things considered, wasn't much of a hiding-place. Anxiously he thrust his property into the pocket of his vague trousers, which, apart from his furry covering of soot, were the only garment he wore.

He peered about him. He could see a fireplace, a dull black arch like the door of a church. The darkness of the chimney drew him powerfully, like home. He began to crawl towards it. A booted leg suddenly thumped down in front of him, barring his way. He tried to go round it. Down came another leg, heavy as a hammer, an inch from his reaching fingers. Desperately he searched for another darkness, even a mousehole . . .

Outside he could hear voices. At any moment now the door would burst open and the big man would come in with Mister Roberts. It was only natural. Mister Roberts was his owner and had his papers. He crept under a table and hid his face in his hands, in case the shining of his eyes gave him away.

The door opened and feet clumped into the room. They stopped and, for a moment, there was silence. Then a voice grunted, 'Is this what you're looking for, Tom Gosling?', and a hand reached down, got hold of Barnacle by the shoulder, and hauled him into view.

The big man was back and looking for him.

'That's the article,' he said, and Barnacle observed with interest that his arm was still bleeding. 'Come here, lad.'

Barnacle scratched his head. Where was Mister Roberts?

'I said, come here,' the big man repeated, and beckoned.

Barnacle, helped by a shove in his rear, obeyed. They went to a pair of blackened pews that stared at one another across a narrow table, like old men thinking.

'Sit yourself down, lad.'

Barnacle sat and the big man sat opposite. Like the pews, they looked at one another. What the big man saw was a mystery; but Barnacle, to his surprise, saw that his companion wasn't such a giant after all. In fact, he wasn't much bigger than Mister Roberts. It was just that there was a feeling of size about him, as if he was no more than the visible part of another, much larger man.

'Landlord!' called out the big man suddenly. 'A glass of brandy, please. The strongest you've got!'

'Coming up, Tom Gosling!' returned the landlord, and Barnacle felt hopeful.

The brandy came, and Mister Gosling, with a reproachful look at Barnacle, poured it over his bleeding arm. Barnacle sighed. 'Bet it tastes better now than when I bit yer, mister,' he said. 'I should ha' waited.'

Mister Gosling raised his eyebrows. Then he called to the landlord again. 'Half a pint of milk, if you've got such a thing!'

Barnacle rubbed his head. The big man puzzled him. He just sat there, with his hands on his knees, like he was wondering whether or not to give Barnacle a clout round the ear. Barnacle couldn't make him out at all. If you was going to clout, you clouted; and if you wasn't, you went to sleep. And another thing. What had happened about Mister Roberts?

'What's your name, lad?' asked Mister Gosling.

''E calls me Barnacle.' Then, with a flicker of pride, Barnacle added, 'It's on account of me amazin' powers of 'oldin' on.'

'Why were you running away . . . Barnacle?'

'I allus makes a run for it when 'e says 'e's goin' to kill me. It's me nature.'

Mister Gosling frowned, but before he could say anything, the milk arrived and was set down on the table, with the information that the landlord had had to rob the cat. Barnacle gazed at the cat's supper distastefully. 'Cor!' he remarked. 'Looks like water what's 'ad a fright!'

Mister Gosling's powerful face twitched with the speck of a smile. It was only a speck, but it had a peculiar effect on Barnacle. Somehow it reminded him of the tiny picture inside the locket. It was nothing like, really, but –

'Drink up, lad,' urged Mister Gosling, and, as Barnacle lifted the white glass to his black face, he said, 'Dirty, ain't you?'

Barnacle put down the glass. 'You're a sharp one, mister,' he said. 'Don't miss nuffink, do you?'

Mister Gosling compressed his lips but did not reply. Instead, he waited for Barnacle to finish his drink before saying, 'It'll be all right for you to go now. And – and the best of luck to you, lad!'

Barnacle stared at him. He'd sooner the big man had clouted him than said that, so calm and easy. He felt a horrible emptiness inside of him, such as he'd never felt before.

'Go on, Barnacle,' muttered Mister Gosling, shifting in his seat. 'Shove off, lad!'

'I s'pose 'e's waitin' out there for me,' said Barnacle, not understanding, but resigned to the way of the world. 'After all, 'e's got me papers, so I s'pose it's right.'

'If you mean your Mister Roberts, Barnacle, you don't have to worry. He's gone.'

''Ow come, mister? What 'appened?'

'Oh, we had words, Barnacle. We had words.'

Barnacle refused to believe it. Words? He'd seen Mister Roberts stand up to words what would have felled a horse. They just bounced off of him. No, it took more than words to shift Mister Roberts. It took something more in the nature of a boot up the arse . . .

'Words, lad, just words,' Mister Gosling assured him, and went on to relate how Mister Roberts had come puffing and panting up to him and inquiring, in a very disagreeable manner, if a boy had just run past, a boy, black as your hat.

'That's me, mister!' cried Barnacle eagerly. ''E allus calls me that! So what 'appened then?'

Mister Gosling smiled the smile of a storyteller whose audience is longing for more. 'So I says to him, "A boy, you say?" And he says to me, "A boy", and shows me his papers to prove it.'

'That's 'im, that's 'im, mister! 'E's allus got 'is papers! What 'appened then?'

Mister Gosling rubbed his hands together in anticipation. He was just coming to the best part of his story and was looking forward to telling it to great effect. 'So I says to him, "I'm sorry to have to tell you, Mister Roberts, but since I've been standing here, no boy has run past me, neither a black one nor a white one nor a green one with purple stripes."'

'And – and 'e believed yer?'

'Why shouldn't he, Barnacle? It was the solemn, Old Bailey truth. You never ran past me, lad. You ran straight into me supper and stayed!'

Mister Gosling beamed. He couldn't help it. He was still surprised and delighted by the quickness of his own wit. And so was the boy. He clapped his hands and grinned all over his black little face.

'And then, mister, what 'appened then?' pleaded Barnacle, not wanting the story to end.

Mister Gosling shook his head and frowned. It seemed that Mister Roberts had not been entirely convinced. In fact, he had gone so far as to call Mister Gosling a liar. To which Mister Gosling had taken exception.

'So I asked him, Barnacle, very quiet-like, if he'd ever heard the old saying that it was lucky to black a sweep's eye.'

'So you did 'it 'im, then?'

'No. He didn't wait. The last I saw of him, he was going like an engine, puffing black smoke.'

'Cor!' breathed Barnacle, gazing at Mister Gosling like he was a king. 'Cor!'

Mister Gosling expanded visibly. He couldn't help it. The boy's admiration warmed him like rum. Then he remembered and shook his head. 'So it's like I told you. He's gone. You can shove off now, lad.'

Barnacle looked at him. No man on earth could have told what the boy was thinking, least of all himself. Mister Gosling scowled and stood up. 'Suit yourself, then,' he grunted. 'I'm off.'

Barnacle stood up. Mister Gosling looked uncomfortable. He muttered something to himself and sat down again. Barnacle sat down. Mister Gosling opened his mouth as if to say something, thought better of it, and stood up. Barnacle did likewise. No word passed between them. Mister Gosling began to walk towards the door. So did Barnacle. Mister Gosling stopped. So did Barnacle. Mister Gosling took another pace, and so did Barnacle.

There was a shifting in the parlour. Heads appeared round the sides of the high-backed pews. Everybody was interested.

'Reminds me,' said somebody, 'of what happened to me once with a stray pup.'

'What happened, then?'

'Poor little runt it were,' said the man who'd had an adventure with a dog, 'left out in the street. I bent down to stroke it and give it a bit of bread.'

'And then?'

'It followed me all the way home.'

'And then?'

For answer, the first speaker pulled on a rope that lay across his knees, and from under the table lumbered a black Newfoundland dog, as big as a horse. It sat down, and man and dog gazed at one another with such mournful and steady affection that it was hard to say who was the captive of whom.

'See what I mean?' said the man.

Mister Gosling swore and stumped outside. And so did Barnacle.

FOUR

Mister Roberts, the man of soot and papers, trudged home; his face was black with coal and gloom. A cart-driver shouted at him to get out of the way or be squashed. He jumped, snarled ungratefully; then, comfortingly, patted his breast pocket in which, like a dropsical lump, was a fat, greasy wallet secured by a rubber band. His papers. He kept them all.

Inside his wallet, grimy, folded and worn as thin as leaves from a lifetime's cuddling, was every single document that had ever concerned him, from his school reports, the record of his own apprenticeship, his rent-book, his licence to sweep chimneys in the boroughs of Westminster and Southwark, right down to the bundle of receipts for his monthly subscription to the Bermondsey Burial Club that entitled him to a resting place in St George's churchyard.

Everything was there, so that, if he was knocked down in the street, there would be no ignorance about him; nothing would be lacking, except life. His corpse would be that of a fully documented citizen, open and above board.

Except for one thing: the certificate of his birth. He didn't have one: not because he hadn't been born, but because that event had taken place before Parliament had invented the Birth Certificate law. So it wasn't his fault. Nevertheless, the lack of a certificate affected him peculiarly. Whenever he saw a magistrate, a lawyer or a policeman, he'd get a queer, panicky feeling that he'd be asked to produce his birth certificate, or be liable to the full severity of the law. Of course his fears were foolish and unreasonable, but then the only time a man is without a foolish and unreasonable fear is when he's dead.

At about nine o'clock he tramped into Newport Court, Soho, where, as his rent book proclaimed, he resided on the top floor of Number Fourteen. He entered the house and stumped up the dingy, stinking stairs, thinking dark thoughts of the grief and humiliation inflicted on him by his horrible boy. He'd kill him, so help him, he would!

He reached his landing and saw, with a thrill of expectation, that a light was shining from under his door. Barnacle had come back! Mister Roberts heaved a sigh of relief; then, fixing his face into a monstrous scowl, he opened the door.

'Where the 'ell–?' he began furiously; and stopped.

The occupant of the room was not a boy, but a man, a square-built man in dark blue, sitting at his table, in his chair, and by the light of his candle.

'I took the liberty, Mister Roberts,' murmured the man, gesturing towards the candle and the table.

''Oo are yer?' demanded Mister Roberts, alarm and indignation boiling up in his breast. 'What are yer doin' 'ere?'

For answer, the man drew the candle towards himself so that black, Satanic shadows invaded his broad, whiskered face.

'Surely you remember me, Mister Roberts?' pursued the visitor, with a curious, whistling edge to his voice.

Mister Roberts did indeed remember him, and a very unwelcome memory it was. He was one of the gents who had been in the room of Barnacle's calamity.

'If you come about that boy, yer honour –'

'Mr Inspector will do,' interposed the gent. 'My name is Mr Inspector Creaker. Save "Your Honour" for the Bench, Mister Roberts.'

A policeman! Instantly Mister Roberts was panic-stricken. Absurdly, ridiculously, he felt convinced that, at any moment, the Inspector was going to ask to see his birth certificate! But it was Mister Roberts's boy that the Inspector was after, for that boy had stolen a valuable article from his lordship's table, and his lordship wanted it back.

'I nearly 'ad 'im,' cried Mister Roberts eagerly, 'not 'alf an hour ago! But 'e give me the slip, the little turd! But it won't be for long, Mr Inspector! They can't 'ide a sweep's boy for ever!'

'Oh? And who can't hide a sweep's boy for ever, Mister Roberts?' asked the Inspector, the whistle at the edge of his voice growing sharper and setting Mister Roberts's nerves on the rack.

'There was this dirty great ruffian standin' outside of a public 'ouse in one of them narrer streets back of Charin' Cross,' gabbled Mister Roberts, desperately anxious to oblige. ' 'E knew where 'e was, I'll take me Bible oath!'

'What public house?'

'The Jolly Bargeman, it were.'

'And you think he went inside?'

'Like I said, me Bible oath, Mr Inspector, sir!'

'No need for that. Your word is good enough, Mister Roberts. I can see that you're an honest man. I know that you would never harbour a thief.'

'I never knew 'e was like that, Mr Inspector! As Gawd's me witness, I took 'im on in good faith! Look, look! 'Ere's 'is papers!'

Mister Roberts, sweating through his soot, dragged out his wallet and, with shaking hands, began to fumble through its contents. He could feel the Inspector's eye watching him, watching his papers . . .

' 'Ere! 'Ere it is!' he cried, finding the document and thrusting it under the Inspector's nose. 'Absalom Brown, that's 'im – '

'Absalom Brown, eh?' murmured the Inspector, glancing at the paper. 'Was not Absalom the young man in the Bible who was hanged by his hair? An unlucky name to give a boy. Absalom Brown. I'll remember that.'

'Like a animal, that's what 'e is!' warned Mister Roberts, thankfully bundling up his wallet and putting it away. 'Like a wild animal!'

'Like a wild animal?' mused the Inspector. 'Well, well! We all know what must be done with wild animals, don't we, Mister Roberts?'

'Put 'em behind bars, eh?'

'That's right, Mister Roberts,' smiled the Inspector, rising to his feet. 'We must put them where they can't do any harm.' He walked to the door.

' 'E bites, Mr Inspector! Watch 'im, or 'e'll bite!'

'I'll bear it in mind, Mister Roberts. He bites,' said the Inspector, leaving the room and beginning to descend the stairs.

'You can't miss 'im, Mr Inspector!' shouted Mister Roberts after his departing visitor. ' 'E's as black as yer 'at!'

The footsteps halted. 'I'll remember, Mister Roberts,' came the Inspector's voice. 'He's as black as your hat.'

The footsteps resumed. The sweep waited until he heard the front door open and then shut. He heaved a sigh of relief and slumped into an ancient, battered easy chair. He fidgeted, but it was no good. The chair had changed its nature and become distinctly uneasy. He stared unhappily at a dirty straw mattress that was heaped up against a wall.

'Well, you brung it on yerself, Barnacle,' he mumbled. 'You done yerself in the eye this time!'

Mister Roberts was not a bad man, nor was he a particularly good one. He was just a man like any other man, plagued and corrupted by a foolish and unreasonable fear.

Inspector Creaker walked swiftly and purposefully towards Charing Cross. He was familiar with the Jolly Bargeman, where he was both feared and respected as a stern but upright officer of the law.

A policeman on the corner of St Martin's Lane saluted him. He returned the greeting and inquired if the constable had lately seen a boy, a running, or a lurking boy, 'black as your hat'. The constable thought for a moment, then shook his head. The Inspector walked on.

Although outwardly he was calm and in command of himself, inwardly there was uncertainty. He knew that he had been to blame for the boy's escape, and, try as he might to hide it from himself, he knew the reason why. It was the sudden sight of the locket in the boy's hand, and the look in the boy's eyes, that had made him hesitate. He had been unpleasantly reminded of other eyes, likewise filled with fear and hate, that had stared back at him before so foolishly vanishing into the darkness of a dead end.

His superiors had noticed his lapse. 'You hesitated, Inspector. You let him get away.'

The reproach, though spoken softly, had stung the Inspector like a slap in the face. He knew that he had failed in his duty both to his country and to himself. He was determined to make amends.

He crossed the Strand and walked briskly down Villiers Street, stopping once or twice to investigate, with boot or truncheon, boy-sized shadows in doorways; then he turned into Duke Street, where the sign of the Jolly Bargeman creaked and glimmered on the left-hand side. He paused outside, glanced up and down the street, then, negligently swinging his truncheon, went inside.

There was a general peering of faces round the sides of the high-backed pews; then a general lowering of looks and spirits when it was seen who the newcomer was. The Inspector shrugged his shoulders. He was used to being unwelcome; but at the same time he felt that there was a disappointment in the air, as if someone else had been expected.

'I'm looking for a boy,' he said, walking between the pews and looking from side to side. 'A sweep's boy. Been in here, so I'm told.' Heads were shaken, slowly, thoughtfully, then eyes, which had avoided his, fixed themselves stonily, obstinately, on tankards of beer. 'Witness ready to swear on his Bible oath,' went on the Inspector, reaching the end of the room and turning back. 'Come, now, gentlemen . . .'

'Sweep's boy, you say, Mr Inspector?' suddenly inquired a customer, beside whom the Inspector had paused.

'That's right,' said the Inspector, encouragingly. 'A sweep's boy.'

'Thin as a drink of water?' pursued the customer, with a reminiscent twinkle in his eye.

'You could say so.'

'And black as a shadow, with eyes?'

'That's him!'

'Then I ain't seen 'im, Mr Inspector,' said the customer, hastily hiding his grin in his beer.

There was a subdued chuckling in the room, and the Inspector himself ventured a smile. 'Now what have we here?' he asked, affably regarding the humorist. 'A witty gentleman, as I live and breathe! Well, I like a joke as well as the next man. Nothing wrong with a joke. It ain't against the law.' His gaze roamed over the customer, then settled on his tankard of beer, beside which, like a large black beetle, lay the customer's hat. 'So we'll wink at that one and I'll say again,' the Inspector went on, still smiling, 'a sweep's boy. Been in here. You couldn't have missed him. Black as – as YOUR HAT!' With a sudden smashing blow he brought down his truncheon on the table. When he took it away, the customer stared in dismay at the ruins of his hat.

'I'm after a boy,' repeated the Inspector, and the Jolly Bargeman held its breath, 'black as . . . your hat.'

FIVE

A boy, white as a chicken bone, stood outside St Marylebone Public Baths, trying to hold up his trousers, which hung on him, loose as cobwebs. Although the night was warm, Barnacle, like Adam before him, felt his nakedness and shivered. Mister Gosling, standing beside him, saw the shiver and sighed wearily. 'There!' he said, taking off his own waistcoat and draping it round the boy's sharp, skinny shoulders.

Barnacle submitted, but was not impressed. It would have needed a deal more than a kindly waistcoat to restore the big man in his esteem. Mister Gosling had done unto him worse, even, than Mister Roberts. And that was saying a mouthful. He had pitched the screaming, shrieking boy into a tub of steaming water and cruelly assaulted him with a scouring brush and soap; and then, when Barnacle had naturally tried to bite the hand that scrubbed him, he had meanly interposed the brush, so Barnacle had broken a tooth. Tenderly he explored the sharp edge with his tongue.

'Come along, lad,' said Mister Gosling, laying a powerful hand on his shoulder, and drawing him along.

Barnacle went. He had no choice. He was too weak from his recent experience to do anything but trudge and stumble by the big man's side.

'What have you got there, Tom Gosling?' called out a voice

from the night. 'Bait for the fishes, or a bit of supper for the cat?'

A policeman loomed into view, with a grin like a rusty saw.

'I don't rightly know, Mister Rook,' returned Tom Gosling, pausing and scratching his head. 'But you could say that he's like one of them sausages from the Jolly Bargeman: an unwholesome mystery inside of a skin.'

The policeman laughed and loomed away; and Barnacle and Tom Gosling walked on. From time to time the boy peered up and tried to read the big man's intentions from the expression on his face; but each time he did so, he found that Mister Gosling was peering down, apparently with the same idea. So they both looked the other way, and remained mysterious to each other.

'Wotcher goin' to do wiv me, mister?' croaked Barnacle, horribly, for his throat was still sore from screaming and his tongue was sour and slimy from bath-house soap.

'Set you to work, my lad,' said Mister Gosling, 'I suppose.'

'You can't do that, mister!'

'Oh! And why not, Barnacle? Are you frightened of work?'

'I'm frightened of everythin', mister,' answered Barnacle, truthfully. 'It's me nature, see? Anyway, you ain't got me papers.'

'Ah, but I've got you, lad, and that's enough for me!' said Mister Gosling firmly, as if, by washing alone, and without a paper or a penny changing hands, Barnacle had passed into his ownership. Barnacle felt indignant.

'Mister Roberts'll 'ave the law on you, mister!'

'He'll have to find you first! And by the look of you now, Barnacle, your own mother wouldn't know you!'

'Don't suppose she ever did, mister,' muttered Barnacle, suddenly sullen and subdued.

'Don't you remember her?'

'Orfigen boy, that's me. I'm yer waif, yer bit of 'uman driftwood . . . object of charity, mister,' said Barnacle, whose amazing powers of holding on were by no means confined to brickwork but included an astonishing variety of odds and ends of words and expressions he'd picked up in the dark course of his chimney life. 'Child of sin.'

Mister Gosling halted. They were in a steep, dark street that led down towards the river. The air smelled of old wood, old stone and old fish, and the invisible water mumbled and muttered. Mister Gosling stared down at Barnacle, almost wonderingly. 'But you must have had a mother . . . a home, maybe?'

True enough. Mister Gosling was a sharp one all right. Somewhere, in the blackness of time past, Barnacle must have had a mother. It stood to reason. But who and what she had been was beyond him. Indeed, if he'd been told that he'd been hatched out of an egg in the Orphanage cellar, he wouldn't have been altogether surprised. But still, it was plain that the big man expected an answer, so Barnacle did his best.

'Well, if you puts it like that, mister, and now I comes to think on it,' he began with an earnest air, 'it was the gipsies wot nicked me.' He paused, having temporarily run out of ideas. Mister Gosling waited, one eyebrow up and the other down. 'I remembers a 'ouse,' Barnacle continued thoughtfully, 'a dirty great manshun wiv 'undreds of skivvies . . .', and then, feeling that still more was expected of him, suddenly recollected twelve brothers who had sold him to an old woman who had shoved him up a chimney. 'There!' he finished up, gazing at Mister Gosling with shining sincerity and the remains of soap all over his face. ' 'Ow's that, mister?'

Mister Gosling slowly shook his head. 'Try again, Barnacle,' he said.

Barnacle shrugged his shoulders. 'All right, mister. 'Ow about this? Bucken'am Palace. Found on the doorstep. Prince o' Wales fevvers in me 'and. Straight up, mister! Cross me 'eart and 'ope to git stuck up a soap biler's flue if I tells a lie!'

Mister Gosling sighed, but did not invite Barnacle to try again; and Barnacle, feeling he had come off best, sniffed and gave a defiant hitch to his trousers.

Mister Gosling looked at him with sudden curiosity. 'What have you got in there, lad?'

The big man had sharp ears. He had heard a faint clink of metal on metal.

'Nuffink, mister. It were just me bones chimin' together.'

'Show me.'

'What? Me bones?'

'I said, show me!' repeated the big man, holding out his hand and frowning menacingly. 'Or do you want me to hold you upside down and shake you?'

He meant it all right. Barnacle could see himself being jerked and shaken till his eyes and teeth flew out all over the street. Whimpering miserably, he produced all that was left of his property: the silver spoon and the golden locket. Mister Gosling stared at them, but made no move to take them away.

'Where did you steal them from?'

'I never stealed nuffink, mister!' wailed Barnacle, vigorously shaking his head so that the tears that stood in his eyes flew out.

'That spoon. It's silver. Where did you get it?'

'I was born wiv it, mister! Straight up! I was born wiv it in me mouf!'

'And the locket? Born with it round your neck, I suppose!'

'It – it were me muvver's, mister!' cried Barnacle, his voice rising to a hoarse little scream of anxiety, for the locket was peculiarly precious to him. 'It were the last thing she gave me . . . afore she snuffed it! Look, mister!' With trembling fingers he opened the locket and displayed the tiny picture within. 'Look 'ere! See! It – it's me an 'er . . . when I was little!'

Mister Gosling drew in his breath harshly. Then he looked from the pea-sized mother and child to the child-sized child.

For a moment, there was an odd solemnity in his face. Then he shook his head. 'Oh, Barnacle, Barnacle! Ain't there no end to your lies?'

'No more'n there is to me, mister,' muttered the boy. 'Come to the end of one an' you comes to the end of the other . . . as the 'angman said to 'is customer when 'e tied the rope an' measured 'im fer the drop. Anyways, what's it to you?'

'What indeed, lad!' sighed Mister Gosling, after a moment's fruitless thought. 'Come along. We're nearly home.'

Barnacle felt better. No effort had been made to deprive him of his property, so he put it back in his pocket and followed the big man down the street.

At the end of the street were two iron posts that stood at the head of a flight of steep stone steps. Beyond them lay Mister Gosling's world. It was a dark and mysterious world, where the cobbles were as big as stone loaves. It was full of creakings and mutterings and looming warehouses with jutting hoists that dripped with hooks and ropes, like iron noses that had sneezed.

Mister Gosling halted and, gripping Barnacle's shoulder with one hand, he pointed with the other. 'There she is, lad,' he said proudly. 'The *Lady*. The *Lady of the Lea*.'

For a moment, Barnacle's heart lifted as he entertained the vision of a Mrs Gosling, warm and lovely as cushions in the dark. Then, when he saw what Mister Gosling was pointing to, his feelings underwent a sudden change. His eyes grew huge with alarm. 'But – but it's floatin', mister! It's a bleedin' boat! Oh Gawd, ain't I 'ad enough of water?'

SIX

Mr Inspector Creaker walked the night. Street after uneasy street heard the steady tread of his square-toed boots; corner after peeping corner watched his thickset shape as it passed through yellow pools of lamplight, and vanished beyond. Passers-by, late home-goers, reeking revellers and the frightened poor hid their sins under strained smiles, muttered, 'Good night . . . good night, Mr Inspector, sir,' and hurried away.

He walked along the Strand as far as Fleet Street, turned down towards Blackfriars, and threaded his way back towards the Jolly Bargeman. Then he retraced his steps, pausing at every darkened doorway and listening intently for the tell-tale sound of quick, shallow breathing . . .

'I'm looking for a boy, a sweep's boy . . . black as your hat.'

A constable, leaning against a wall and lost in private dreams, jerked upright as the Inspector addressed him.

'A boy, Mr Inspector, sir?'

'That's right. Black as your hat.'

The constable pondered, then suggested a certain cellar under the railway arch off Bridge Street, where vagrant infants congregated for the night. The Inspector nodded and followed the constable. Presently they came to a grim-looking hole in a grim brick wall. The constable shone his lantern and revealed stairs descending steeply into blackness. 'Anybody new down there?'

A moment's shuffling silence, then a voice, thin as a bird's, replied: 'No, mister. We're all old down 'ere.'

The constable went down a step or two and his lantern explored the darkness. Faces appeared, belonging, by their size, to children – little grey and yellow faces, bewildered by the light, and blasted with poverty and hate. After a moment, the constable doused his light and the darkness flooded back; but the faces remained, printed on the inner eye. The Inspector frowned, shook his head, and walked away.

He returned to the Jolly Bargeman and from there made his way to the Embankment. He walked along slowly and with frequent pauses, during which he stared thoughtfully over the parapet into the black waters of the river. Presently he was joined by a shadowy figure who had flitted across the road opposite Somerset Stairs. For a few moments the two murmured together, then the shadow departed, as noiselessly as it had come. The Inspector walked on.

He came to an ugly little public house near Charing Cross, leaking dirty light like a disease. He went inside, glanced round the dim and smoky room and then seated himself at a table where there was a portly, red-faced man who was studiously peeling an apple with a small bright knife. As with the shadow, murmurs were exchanged, after which the Inspector rose and departed, while the red-faced man smiled to himself and went on with peeling his apple.

Two more such establishments were visited, and an actors' doss-house off Drury Lane, where similar murmurings took place, murmurings with queer, quiet individuals, some of whom looked more like thieves and cut-throats than the associates of so stern and upright an officer as Mr Inspector Creaker.

But they were policemen too, shadow policemen, policemen on the other side of the light. Nobody, except for Inspector Creaker, knew for certain who they were or where they were to be found, for they were the secret police. They were dangerous men, with all the subtle skills of murderers; but they were dangerous only to enemies of the State. It was their sworn duty to hunt down and destroy the assassins, the bomb-throwers, the stirrers-up of unrest in the streets . . . often men from abroad who came ashore from ships by night, and sought to overthrow the established order of the nation. They were secret because their enemies were secret; they were ruthless because their enemies were ruthless. They fought fire with fire, deceit with deceit, and murder with murder. But whatever they did was done for the security of the State.

In all, there were some dozen of them, scattered about like needles in the dark. They were under the command of Inspector Creaker, behind whom stood certain shadowy Ministers of the Crown. It was from these Ministers that the Inspector derived his power; it was to them that he owed his allegiance and, such was his unswerving loyalty, his life itself. Consequently he could never forgive himself for having failed in the affair of the sweep's boy and the enormously important gold locket; and, until the locket was recovered and the boy silenced, he could never be at peace with himself. There was no middle way with Inspector Creaker. He was a man with no twilight in his soul.

He walked down Drury Lane and into the Strand. A street lamp on the opposite side of the road attracted a constable who had loomed out of nowhere, like a bulky, helmeted moth. He stood, fidgeting solemnly with the lantern at his belt. The Inspector crossed the road and approached. The constable saluted.

'I'm looking for a boy, Mister Rook,' said the Inspector, recognizing the man.

'Oh, and what manner of boy, Mr Inspector, sir?'

'A sweep's boy, Mister Rook.'

'Very skinny, were he, Mr Inspector, no more'n eyes and bone?'

'Could be, Mister Rook. A skinny boy, black as your hat.'

'Not the one, then, Mr Inspector, sir. The one I saw were as white as a chicken bone.'

'That's a pity, Mister Rook.'

'He were,' went on the constable, anxious to impress his superior with his powers of observation, 'in the words of the individual what was with him, like one of them sausages in the Jolly Bargeman: an unwholesome mystery inside of a skin.'

'The Jolly Bargeman, you said?' inquired the Inspector, sharply.

'The Jolly Bargeman *he* said,' corrected the constable.

'Indeed? And who might he be?'

'Name of Thomas Gosling, Mr Inspector, sir. A bargee what ties up at Broken Wharf. Vessel by the name of the *Lady of the Lea*.'

'And this chicken bone of a boy went off with him?'

'That he did, sir.'

'In your opinion, Mister Rook, were they well acquainted with one another?'

'In my opinion, Mr Inspector, sir,' returned the constable, expanding and waxing eloquent, 'they'd scarce had time to breathe off each other the frost of perfect strangers. Why, with me own ears I heard the boy inquire, "What are you going to do with me, mister?" '

The Inspector's heart beat fast, and he smiled a small, grim smile. 'Thank you, Mister Rook. You're a sharp fellow and I'll not forget you.'

'I do no more than me duty, sir,' murmured the constable, modestly.

'And no man need do more, Mister Rook,' said the Inspector. 'Mister Gosling, you say?'

'That's right, sir, Tom Gosling of the *Lady of the Lea*.'

'And Broken Wharf, you say?'

'That's right, Mr Inspector, sir. Tied up at –'

But before the constable could finish, the Inspector had gone. The constable sighed and shrugged his shoulders, and gently loomed away.

Broken Wharf was dark and quiet, and the tottering warehouses poked their iron noses uselessly into the business of the night. Here and there, huge hooks hung in the air, like upside-down question-marks: Where is he? Where? Where?

Sombrely the Inspector stared at them. He stood at the water's edge. The mooring was empty. The barge had gone.

SEVEN

Barnacle in the dark. Cautiously, suspiciously, he sniffed. He shook his head. There was no comfortable, sneezing smell of private soot; there was no easy stink of stale beer, stale pork and stale Mister Roberts. All the old familiar smells were gone. In their place was the tickling, prickling odour of a strange blanket, a strange bed and strange company.

He listened. Even the sounds were different and uneasy. He could hear the sighs and mutters of nearby water, and the ticking and grunting of straining wood. From no more than an arm's reach away he could hear the steady snores of Mister Gosling and, a little further off, the gentle chiming of jugs and saucepans as they swung against each other, keeping time with the wobbling of the barge.

He opened an eye, but very secretly, as if the noise of his eyelid would betray him. He saw the dim and glinting interior of Mister Gosling's residence. A small brown box, furnished. He opened the other eye. He saw the door. Grey light peeped and glimmered round its edges. It was morning outside.

Soundlessly and with infinite care he emerged from his blanket, like a climbing boy from a stealthy chimney-pot. He waited. Then he crawled out of the long, narrow drawer in the cabin's wall where sailors were folded away for the night.

He waited again, then climbed down, pausing on the way to peer into the drawer below, which was full of the sleeping Mister Gosling. As he gazed at the rising and falling shape, he felt vaguely disturbed, as if he had eaten something that had disagreed with him. He licked his lips and swallowed, but the sensation remained. It was guilt. He knew that the big man had meant kindly by him. Mister Gosling was, as grown men went, a peaceable gent. Most likely, when he waked and found that his boy had gone, he would be a little sad. But it was no good. Barnacle was a land animal. He was an animal of the streets and corners and of the private dark of flues. The great rocking river filled him with terror and dismay.

'I likes a bit o' fish for me supper,' he muttered as he drifted, like a bony little ghost, towards the door, 'but I don't aim to be a bit o' supper for the bleedin' fish! So it's goodbye, mister . . . and thanks . . .'

He opened the door and began to mount the steep stairway that led up to the hatch. At every step he stopped and listened. The big man's breathing remained steady and undisturbed. He reached the hatch and pushed. Inch by inch it opened, and inch by inch Barnacle's head rose above the barge's deck, like a wart, growing. For a moment, he was aware of a strangeness, a hugeness of air. He took another step, and –

'A-a-a-a-ah!' he screamed. From nowhere a hook like an iron policeman's finger had seized him by the neck of Mister Gosling's waistcoat and dragged him off his feet!

Howling and shrieking, he fought and twisted and struggled; but there was no escape. The grip on his neck was murderous, and the harder he tried to free himself, the worse it became. At length he lay still, panting and sobbing, face down on the deck.

'That's more like it,' said the unseen wielder of the hook. 'you keep still or I'll poke your guts out!'

Fearfully he twisted his head in order to see the extent of his misfortune. He saw that the hook that had caught him was at the end of a long wooden pole. At the other end of it, crouching on an adjoining barge, was a glaring female demon with furious hair and blazing eyes. She was about fourteen . . .

'Ma!' screeched the demon triumphantly. 'Ma! Come'n see what I caught!'

Barnacle twitched. Instantly the hook tightened and caused him intense pain. He howled and gave up.

'Ma! Ma!' shouted the demon impatiently. 'Hurry up, you old bag!'

The old bag appeared. She billowed up out of a hatch and stood, swaying and heaving and clutching a frying pan: a demon of the larger size.

'I'll give you "old bag", miss!' she bellowed, outraged, and shook her frying pan like a huge black fist.

She was a roaring, mighty figure of a woman, firmly upholstered, like a sea-going sofa. Here and there, there were splits in her attire, with something very like stuffing poking through, as if she had seen some use. But her hair was her amazement and glory. It was red and all over curl-papers, as if a cloud of butterflies had alighted on a burning bush.

The girl regarded her with satisfaction. 'I knew that'd fetch you up quick, ma,' she said. 'Look what I caught!'

The old bag looked, and Barnacle shrank before her stare. The girl explained: 'I hooked him just as he was creeping up out of Uncle Tom's cabin, ma.'

'Mister Gosling's!' shouted the old bag, indignantly. 'Mister Gosling's cabin! How many more times have I got to tell you that he's no relation of ours! Now!' She turned her attention to Barnacle. 'Now, you little river rat, you! You ferrety little runt! What have you been stealing?'

'Nuffink, missus, nuffink!' wailed Barnacle, shutting his eyes and hoping that when he opened them again he'd be back in a chimney. 'Bile me in gravy if I tells a lie!'

'Then let's boil him, ma!' screeched the girl, giving a sharp tug at the hook. 'Look! That's Uncle Tom's weskit he's got on! He's nicked it!'

'Mister Gosling's! I'll put you across my knee if there's any more of that Uncle Tom! Mister Gosling's weskit! And stolen, not nicked! But you're quite right, girl. It's his garment . . . shabby article that it is! MISTER GOSLING!' She raised her voice to the huge dimensions of a fog-horn. 'MISTER GOSLING! Wake up! Wake up! You've been robbed, you lazy loafer, you!'

Thumps and bumps and hoarse cries from below as Mister Gosling, wrenched from sleep, banged his head against the top of his bunk. Then the barge shook as he came lumbering up on to the deck.

'What the devil's happening, Clara?' he began, when the old bag shouted him down.

'Don't you "Clara" me in a public place, Mister Gosling! It's Mrs McDipper, and don't you forget it!'

Hastily the big man apologized; then he saw his boy.

'Good God!' he cried. 'What have you been doing to my poor little Barnacle?'

A moment later, Barnacle felt powerful hands freeing him from the grip of the hook.

'It's all right, lad, it's all right!'

Disbelievingly, Barnacle opened his eyes. He saw Mister Gosling's feet, large and lumpy as raw potatoes. He looked up. The sky was early-morning grey, and Mister Gosling was smiling down. He struggled upright and stared about him. The long, narrow deck was littered with ropes and chains, and the huge red sail was bundled up against the tall mast, as if the *Lady of the Lea* had seen a mouse and clutched her skirts.

The long wooden pole was gone. But it wasn't the only thing that had gone. Barnacle glared about him in bewilderment and terror! The houses were gone. The roofs and chimneys were gone. The very streets were gone. It was if they had all been swept away by a giant's broom, and the emptiness left behind had been painted green. As far as he could see there was a green nothingness, quiet as a cemetery, under the nothingness of a huge grey sky. The barge had sailed while he'd been asleep, sailed right off the edge of the world!

'Where's all the 'ouses an' corners gone?' he wept. 'An' all this screamin' great sky! It ain't natcheral, mister, it ain't natcheral! Fer Gawd's sake take me back to the streets an' chimneys an' fings what I knows!'

'Why, we're just tied up a few miles downriver, lad,' said Mister Gosling comfortingly. 'We'll be sailing back on the turn of the tide.'

'And straight to the lock-up!' said Mrs McDipper firmly. 'He was after stealing your weskit, Mister Gosling, the thieving little brat!'

'Stealing me weskit?' exclaimed Mister Gosling wonderingly. 'Why, bless you, Clara – I mean Mrs McDipper! I put it on him myself! The boy was almost naked. Look for yourself!'

Before Barnacle could prevent him, he'd plucked aside the waistcoat and revealed rather more of Barnacle than was commonly exposed to the public gaze.

Mrs McDipper shrieked. 'Oh! Oh! The shameless little toad! Shut your eyes, Miranda, or I'll shut 'em for you, miss!'

'Come on, ma!' protested Miranda. 'There ain't nothing there even to frighten a holy nun!'

Barnacle shrank before Miranda's contemptuous gaze and covered himself up. He felt a great surge of bitterness against a world that regarded him with such disgust. 'I were decent,' he mumbled miserably, 'afore I were washed.'

Mrs McDipper sniffed. 'Where did you get him, Gosling?' she demanded, as if Barnacle was a thing and not a person.

'He was a sweep's boy on the run,' explained Mister Gosling, and went on to tell of the momentous meeting outside the Jolly Bargeman.

Fascinated, Barnacle listened to the events related from the big man's point of view, of how Mister Gosling had been gazing up at the stars and thinking of Mrs McDipper when, all of a sudden, he was struck in the supper by a small black, flying and biting article, no better than a frightened animal.

'A good deal worse, I should say,' commented Mrs McDipper, and, to Barnacle's indignation, Mister Gosling agreed.

'But when he was washed,' went on Mister Gosling, 'I got the surprise of me life! He came up as bright as a shilling. Why, his own mother wouldn't have known him!'

He paused and frowned slightly, as if uncertain of how to go on. Barnacle wondered if he was thinking about the picture in the locket, of 'me ma an' me when I was little'. But he never said anything about the locket or the silver spoon. Perhaps he was being careful? Perhaps he was frightened that if the McDippers knew about Barnacle's property, they'd nick it or tell the police?

Mrs McDipper put down her frying-pan and began to pace the deck of her barge, which was larger and grander than the *Lady of the Lea*. At length she halted. 'You're a fool, Tom Gosling,' she said. 'You always were and you always will be.' Mister Gosling did not deny it. Mrs McDipper fidgeted with her gown. 'Permission to come aboard, Mister Gosling?'

'Permission granted, ma'am.'

A moment later, and by way of the quayside, she was on the deck of the *Lady of the Lea*, and her daughter was not long after her. Fastidiously, and with little grunts of disapproval, she picked her way among the litter of ropes.

'A word with you, Mister Gosling,' she said as she approached him. 'In private.'

'In me cabin?'

She shook her head. 'Miranda!'

'Yes, ma?'

'Go up to the Traveller's Rest and a fetch back some hot coffee, girl.'

'Right, ma.'

'And Miranda –'

'Yes, ma?'

'Take that – that Barnacle with you. And see he keeps himself decent, I won't have him offending the modesty of young girls.'

'Right, ma.'

'And Miranda –'

'What else, ma?'

'Don't hurry back.'

'Understood, ma.'

The girl approached Barnacle. Uneasily he retreated behind Mister Gosling. The big man stepped aside. The girl shrugged her shoulders, then she beckoned and made a clucking noise. 'Here, boy, here. Come along now. Come to Miranda.'

'I ain't a dog,' mumbled Barnacle, clutching at a tattered shred of dignity, 'miss.'

But he went with her all the same. He had seen Mrs McDipper slip her arm inside Mister Gosling's, and draw him close. He felt cold and unvalued, and no part of anybody's world.

EIGHT

The firm ground felt tilting and unnatural after the motherly rocking of the *Lady of the Lea*, and Barnacle was inclined to roll from side to side as he followed the girl along the cart track that led away from the quayside. From time to time she glanced back at him over her shoulder with a challenging look as if to say: 'Go on! Make a run for it and see how far you get!' Then, apparently satisfied that Barnacle was thoroughly cowed, she transferred her attention to the tall, thick grass that grew on either side of the road.

She began humming to herself, as if she was entirely alone, and picking tiny pink and yellow wild flowers until she had collected a sizeable bunch. Then, ingeniously binding the stems together with a long blade of grass, she skilfully inserted the bouquet into her red hair, and studied the effect in a small mirror that she drew out of a pocket in her gown.

Barnacle watched with interest. He picked a flower she had overlooked and offered it to her. It was hard to say why he did it. Perhaps it was only because of a monkey-like instinct for copying? She looked at him in some astonishment. However, she accepted the tribute and poked it into the bosom of her gown, where it looked as surprised as she.

'How old are you?'

'Dunno, miss,' said Barnacle after thinking it over. 'Twelve or firteen, I s'pose.'

Miranda shook her head. 'Can't be. Ten, more like it. You're too small for thirteen.'

'You 'as to be for chimney work, miss,' said Barnacle, experiencing a sensation of importance. 'Get stuck if you're well growed. Then they 'as to take the wall down to fetch you out. Dead. My Mister Roberts,' he went on reminiscently, 'used ter say, "Barnacle, lad, don't you eat no more. Grow another inch an' you're a goner!"'

'Barnacle!' exclaimed Miranda contemptuously. 'That ain't a name! It's a misfortune to the bottom of a boat!'

Barnacle felt affronted. ''E called me Barnacle on account of me amazin' powers of 'oldin' on.'

'If you were so good at it, why did you run away?'

''E said 'e'd kill me. I allus runs when 'e says that. It's me nature, miss.'

'Oh.'

Nothing further passed between them. Barnacle felt disappointed. He'd hoped to tell the girl about extraordinary adventures in the flues of London, of huge falls of soot and sudden birds as big as horses, and Whistling Edge and Smooth-and-Bony, but she never asked. Apparently her interest in him had been exhausted.

Presently they reached the Traveller's Rest. It was an old and sleepy whitewashed inn, with an untidy thatch, as if it had just woken up and scratched its head. There was a painted sign outside, depicting a merry traveller clutching a tankard overflowing with ale in one hand and a beaming barmaid overflowing her gown with the other. They went up to a side door and Miranda knocked and called: 'Annie. It's me!'

A moment later, the upper half of the door opened and revealed the upper half of Annie, like a picture in a frame, and needing only the merry traveller and the beer to be the spitting image of the sign. She was a real beauty . . .

'You're early, dear,' she said, her voice still thick and croaking from sleep. 'It ain't six o'clock yet.' Then her misty blue eyes swivelled and lighted upon Barnacle. 'What's that you got with you? I ain't seen him before, have I?'

'Name of Barnacle, Annie. Belongs to Mister Gosling.'

'Ah yes,' said Annie with a dreamy smile. 'I thought I recognized his weskit. Poor little mite! He looks just like an old umbrella with all them ribs and folds. Jug of coffee, dear?'

Miranda nodded and Annie, after another long look at Mister Gosling's waistcoat, went away. Miranda, still not interested in Barnacle, took out her mirror and fiddled with the flowers in her hair. Barnacle watched her sombrely.

'She don't like me, do she miss?' he said abruptly.

'Who? Annie?'

'No. Your ma.'

Miranda put away her mirror and looked Barnacle up and down, critically but not unkindly. 'Well, you can't blame her, Barnacle. It ain't personal,' she hastened to say, as Barnacle had begun to look even more dejected than usual, 'but you ain't exactly what we want for a neighbour. Your Mister Gosling's bad enough.'

'What's wrong with 'im, miss? I thought your ma was sweet on 'im.'

Miranda sighed. 'Life ain't as simple as that, Barnacle. There's things a sweep's boy could never understand . . . like – like class.'

'Do you mean winders, miss?' asked Barnacle eagerly. He knew all about windows –

'*Class*,' said Miranda irritably, 'not glass. Class. Social position, my lad.'

She paused. Barnacle looked at her expectantly, but it was plain that he was out of his depth.

'Listen, Barnacle,' she said patiently, 'and I'll try to explain. We – that's me and me ma – own our barge. It's all ours. It's our property, and when me ma pops her clogs, it'll be mine. But your Mister Gosling doesn't own the *Lady of the Lea*. He only rents it. Every Monday morning he has to go to the owners' office and pay his rent, like a common tenant. And if ever he didn't have the money, they'd turn him off the barge and he wouldn't be worth a spit in the wind.' She paused again, then she said softly, 'So you see, Barnacle, until Uncle Tom saves up enough money to buy the *Lady* for himself, there can't ever be anything between him and my ma but a cold slice of the River Thames. Now do you understand?'

Barnacle lowered his head and stared at his feet. He didn't understand. He was a simple soul and the complications of living baffled him. Once more he longed for what he knew: the darkness of chimneys and the comfort of soot . . .

'Sugar, dear?'

Annie was back, with a steaming jug and a huge piece of bread and dripping.

'For that little mite,' she said, and gave it to Barnacle. Then she began to spoon in sugar in response to Miranda's nod. 'It's a shame,' she said, casting glances at Mister Gosling's waistcoat. 'Ain't that poor little mite got nothing of his own to wear?'

Miranda shrugged her shoulders.

'I got fings of me own,' said Barnacle, suddenly wanting to be thought better of by the present company. 'Only – only I come away sudden, didn't I? I got a proper jacket and anuvver pair of trahsers, ain't I? I got real boots an' a green weskit and – and I 'ad a 'at once, wiv a brass badge, didn't I?'

'I don't know, Barnacle,' said Miranda, staring at him curiously. 'Did you?'

He shut his mouth. He had shot his bolt, and missed. He felt angry. Miranda took the jug and they walked back towards the river in silence. The morning was growing brighter, but Barnacle wasn't. He trudged along, a private night in the public day. Several times he thought of mentioning his locket and spoon, and even showing them as real evidence that he was worth more than a spit in the wind. But he didn't. Somehow he felt that they were a secret between him and Mister Gosling, and that to share a secret with the big man raised Barnacle a little . . .

When they got to the river, there was company. The quiet green had woken up. The sermon of sleep was over and the congregation was up and about. The little quayside was crowded with lumbering carts and mountainous horses, creaking and steaming and jingling, while a dozen burly labourers, bursting out of their shirts, heaved and staggered and sweated across the quay. The barges were being loaded: bulging sacks aboard the McDippers' vessel and bundles of hay for the *Lady*, piled up high as Ludgate Hill.

'There's work up there for a climbing boy!' called out Mister Gosling as Barnacle and Miranda approached. ''Specially for a boy with amazing powers of holding on!'

Barnacle looked up, alarmed, and Mister Gosling explained that it would be one of his tasks, when he'd learned his starboard from his port, to perch up on high and guide the *Lady* through the mazes of shipping when they sailed back up the Thames. But not to worry. For the first time or two there'd be a Jack-at-a-Pinch sitting up there beside him to show him what was what, and which was his right and which was his left.

'There, Mrs McDipper!' he said proudly. 'In next to no time, my Barnacle will be earning his keep! Think of the money I'll save! Why, in next to no time I'll be a man of property!'

'And what, might I ask,' inquired Mrs McDipper coldly,

'would a hulking great loafer like you want with being a man of property?'

He smiled and shook his head. Miranda dug Barnacle in the ribs in order to exchange a meaning glance with him. For some reason Barnacle felt uncomfortable and didn't know where to look. Then he remembered he was still holding Annie's bread and dripping, so he buried his face in it and began to munch.

'Don't you eat no more, Barnacle,' said Miranda, warningly.

'Why not, miss?'

'Grow another inch and you're a goner.'

He stared at her wonderingly. Her eyes were sparkling and suddenly she laughed.

'What are you laughing at, Miranda?' demanded her mother, suspiciously.

'Nothing, ma. Just something between me and Barnacle.'

Barnacle beamed. For the first time in his life he felt that, all things considered, and taking the rough with the smooth, it was better to be alive than dead. Much better!

NINE

Mr Inspector Creaker lived, when he was not more importantly engaged, very respectably in Dock Street, a long narrow thoroughfare with smoke-blackened tenement buildings on one side and a high brick wall on the other. It was just off Rosemary Lane and a stone's throw from the Tower of London.

Long ago, Dock Street had been known as Saltpetre Bank, on account of gunpowder for the Tower's cannon and for the defence of the Realm having been manufactured and stored there; but although it had changed its gunpowdery name when it had changed its gunpowdery nature, it was still, in the person of Inspector Creaker, devoted heart and soul to the defence of the Realm.

He rented two rooms on the top floor of one of the tenement buildings, and, from one of his windows, he had a good view of the black-capped towers of the old fortress rising up over the intervening roofs and seeming, somewhat fancifully, like fatal judges pronouncing sentence. Often, when he gazed at them, he thought of the many terrible deeds they had looked down on, but always he felt that, however harsh and cruel those deeds had seemed, time had proved them to have been necessary and right. If enemies of the State had not been tortured and had their heads chopped off,

God knew what wickedness would now be ruling the land!

He sighed and, withdrawing his gaze, consulted a ponderous steel watch. The time was exactly half past nine o'clock. He gave another glance out of the window, breathed deeply and, although the morning was warm and bright, put on his heavy caped overcoat and a plain, high-crowned black hat, such as might have been worn by a respectable tradesman. Then, with a careful wipe of a duster over his shining, square-toed boots, he set out from Dock Street and walked briskly towards the City.

His destination, which he reached shortly before ten o'clock, was a stately, grey-stone building near the Mansion House. He mounted the steps and made murmured inquiries at a glass-panelled office just inside the front door. The personage within, after a brief consideration of his ledger, directed the visitor up a flight of red-carpeted stairs and to a handsome door on the right. Hat in hand, the Inspector opened the door and noiselessly went inside.

The room he entered was heavy with the aroma of leather and cigars; and, although there were large windows at one end, the room was so immensely long that the morning light only ventured as far as the fireplace before giving up the ghost and yielding to shadows.

It was quiet, very quiet, as if the room itself was thinking, as if the great chandelier that hung from the ceiling and the mahogany furnishings were all engaged in solemn contemplation. As indeed they might have been; for, although the room was no more than an apartment in a gentlemen's club, it was said that more great decisions had been taken within its walls than ever had been taken in Parliament itself.

There was a gentleman seated in an armchair drawn up by the marble fireplace, and no more animated than either: a thin gentleman with an obstinate fold of fair hair and somewhat staring blue eyes.

'Good morning, Inspector,' he murmured as his visitor approached, and gestured towards an upright chair. He spoke in a voice that an ignorant child might have thought of as smooth and bony.

The Inspector seated himself and placed his hat on the floor beside him. The gentleman rang for a waiter.

'Bring me a glass of brandy,' he ordered when the waiter arrived, 'and – and –' he cast an estimating glance at his visitor, 'a glass of ale, Inspector?'

'Thank you, Mr Hastymite,' returned the Inspector. 'Ale will be very satisfactory.'

The waiter departed and the Inspector leaned forward expectantly.

'A fine day, Inspector, don't you think?' said Mr Hastymite affably.

The Inspector frowned and Mr Hastymite directed a warning glance towards the back of an armchair by the windows. It was inhabited. After a moment of silence, the chair creaked as if Mr Hastymite's look had penetrated the leather and awakened the inhabitant. He stood up. He was a very tall, elderly man with a lugubrious face. The Inspector recognized him as Lord Mounteagle, a once-famous lawyer who had retired from the Bar in order to devote himself to politics. He folded his newspaper, tucked it under his arm and walked towards the door. On his way he paused to address his fellow club member. 'Ah! Hastymite! How goes the Ministry? Ever watchful, eh? Ever guarding us against being blown up in our beds?'

He laughed, and, with the briefest of glances at the Inspector, left the room. Mr Hastymite sighed.

'There goes a very wealthy man. I'm afraid that the profession of law offers richer rewards than does serving one's country, Inspector,' he said with a rueful smile, 'like you and me.'

The Inspector shrugged his shoulders. He had never given

much thought to such matters. The waiter returned with the ale and brandy, and when he had gone Mr Hastymite raised his glass. 'Confusion to our enemies, Inspector!'

'Confusion to our enemies, sir,' echoed the Inspector, and drank.

'Now for your news, Inspector,' said Mr Hastymite, putting down his glass. His languid air was set aside, revealing a sharpness and a strong concern that the Inspector very much respected. 'The boy. Have you caught him?'

'No, sir. Not yet.'

'It was a great pity that you let him get away from you, Inspector. It may even turn out to have been a tragedy.'

'I – I am sorry, sir.'

'Then you had better tell me what you do have to report. Is there any further news of the *December Rose*?'

'She is due in at Deptford on Saturday, the twenty-third, sir.'

'That leaves very little time.'

'She will be watched –'

'Yes, yes! I know that. But you must remember, Inspector, that we are not dealing with fools. We are dealing with exceedingly cunning men. We are dealing with spies, anarchists, socialists, with enemies of the State, man!'

'I know that, sir.'

'Then why, in God's name, did you allow that boy to escape you with the locket? Why, why?'

The Inspector made no reply. He stared straight ahead of him. The sudden harshness in Mr Hastymite's voice was as nothing compared with the harshness with which the Inspector judged himself . . .

'You know the consequences, of course?'

The Inspector nodded. He knew the consequences very well. The loss of the locket had been a disaster. There was a messenger aboard the *December Rose* bringing in funds for the use of a group of dangerous men. He was to hand over the money to a certain woman he would know by the locket she would be wearing.

But now there would be no meeting and no handing over. The woman was dead and the locket was lost.

'The man will be followed, sir,' muttered the Inspector. 'He won't escape us.'

Mr Hastymite compressed his already thin lips, until they were no more than a grim, dark line.

'I told you, Inspector, we are not dealing with fools. Almost certainly he'll leave the funds aboard the ship until he's made sure of the meeting. And I need hardly tell you, Inspector, that if we don't lay our hands on that money, it will find its way into other hands, hands that will put it to the most terrible and horrible use! You must find that boy with the locket, Inspector. You must find him!'

'He will be found, sir. I am confident of that.'

Mr Hastymite nodded. Then he leaned forward and, putting his fingertips together, spoke softly into the little church he had made: 'Found and silenced, Inspector. Silenced. God knows what that little animal might have heard when he was in the chimney. We are fighting secret men, Inspector, and our best weapon is secrecy. We must keep it at all costs.'

'I understand, sir. The boy will be dealt with. He will not get away from me a second time.'

Mr Hastymite relaxed a little. After all, the Inspector, in spite of his one lapse, was a very loyal and trustworthy man . . .

'Do you know, Inspector,' he said, with an air of putting the man at his ease, 'I shall never forget the look on that boy's face when you hesitated. Why, it might almost have been his birthday!' He laughed. 'But that's all in the past, eh, Inspector? Now what we must set our minds to is putting a stop to his birthdays!'

'As I said, sir, the boy will be dealt with.' The Inspector's face was stern. There was no mistaking his resolve, or his ability to carry it out.

'I know it is an unpleasant duty, Inspector,' murmured Mr Hastymite, with unexpected kindness, 'but I am glad to see that you don't flinch from it.'

'Thank you, sir,' said the Inspector, picking up his hat and rising from his chair.

'I'm afraid,' went on Mr Hastymite, 'that we poor devils who serve our country are not as lucky as – as Lord Mounteagle. Our only reward is in knowing that we have done our duty. And sometimes that duty is very, very hard.'

The Inspector glanced involuntarily towards the window. He was thinking of the black-capped towers of the old fortress that had stood, upright and unmoved, through the centuries of blood and screams. Time had proved them right . . .

'It's a pity about that boy, Inspector,' said Mr Hastymite, finishing off his glass of brandy. 'But, after all, he's a small price to pay.'

TEN

The small price was as happy as a flea in a mattress. He was back upriver again, where the houses were; and the *Lady* had stolen his heart. High up on her hill of hay, with the wind rushing by, and her great red sail blowsing out behind him, Barnacle had had a time the Lord Mayor of London would have given his dinner and chain for! He'd danced and bowed to the wandering steeples, he'd screeched mortal insults down on every vessel that passed, and he'd learned his starboard from his port. Surely a climbing boy had never climbed higher than he!

And now he was to be dressed proper, in real clothes bought in a real shop. The old bag – Mrs McDipper – had said something had to be done, so Mister Gosling, bless his tin moneybox, had said he'd lay out five shillings if Mrs McDipper would spend them in Solomon Levy's on Barnacle's behalf. He'd sooner she did the business than he, as she could twist old Levy round her little finger and get more for five shillings than anyone from Richmond to Tilbury Docks.

Soon after midday, when the *Lady* had been unloaded and Mister Gosling had got his money, they were on their way to old Levy's, where Mrs McDipper was to meet them outside. She'd declined to go with them, as she swore she wouldn't be caught dead walking in public with Barnacle in his present indecent state.

Solomon Levy's Used Clothes Emporium was a leaning, bulging premises on the corner of Dorset Street, and painted a fading blue. He described himself as a Nautical Outfitter, and was famous among sailors from Wapping to the China Seas. He did business with deck-hands and pursers and bo'suns and harpooners and seafarers of every shape and size. He could always find something for everybody, and it was said that old Levy could even dress a Yarmouth kipper – if it had the money to pay. His stock, peered at through his crowded window, was enormous; it stretched from Shetland jerseys and Yankee jackets to Chinese reach-me-downs, still inhabited by slant-eyed moths.

Barnacle and Mister Gosling waited outside. As they stood, watching for Mrs McDipper, Barnacle felt warm and human, and curiously concerned for the big man by his side. He thought about class and ownership and the sadness of hopeless love.

'If you don't mind my sayin' so,' he murmured confidentially, 'you could do better, y'know, mister.'

'What do you mean, Barnacle? Better than what?'

'Than 'er wiv the fryin' pan. I see'd some reely luvly lookers round Covent Garden what you could 'ave for a couple of shillin's, mister.'

'Thank you, Barnacle,' said Mister Gosling coldly. 'I'm much obliged. But Mrs McDipper is as handsome a lady as I've ever laid eyes on, or ever want to.'

'Cor, mister –' began Barnacle, about to cast grave doubts on Mister Gosling's eyesight, when his own eyes widened and his mouth fell open in amazement. 'Cor!' he breathed. 'Look at that! It's the bleedin' Queen of Sheba!'

It was Mrs McDipper. But it was a Mrs McDipper such as Barnacle had never dreamed of. It was a Mrs McDipper translated into the language of glory. Sharply nipped in at the waist, she was as magnificent above as below. In gorgeous colours and on invisible feet, she flowed along Dorset Street with a tilted garden on her head. Her eyes provoked, her lips conspired, and roses rioted in her cheeks. Who would have thought that the shabby old bag had been carrying about such a treasure inside!

Beside her, and a little behind, walked Miranda, like a sunburst of the smaller sort. She carried a white parasol which she twiddled, like a fury of doves, above her head.

'*Now* you see what I mean, Barnacle?' murmured Mister Gosling, blinking with admiration. 'The McDippers afloat are one thing, but the McDippers ashore are – are . . . well!'

As they drew near, the air was suddenly full of carnations.

'What fayne weather we're having, Mister Gosling,' observed Mrs McDipper, very refined. 'Don't you think?'

'Not half so fine as you, Mrs McDipper!'

Mrs McDipper smiled, radiantly. 'One laikes to be suitable, Mister Gosling,' she admitted. 'One don't care to be conspicuous.'

Mister Gosling fished in his pocket and produced his five shillings. Mrs McDipper glanced at it as if it was an earwig.

'Just slip it into me hand when I turn me back, Mister Gosling. Ay don't wish to be observed taking money from a gentleman in a public place. Ay don't care to make meself conspicuous.'

It was done in a moment. She turned round, fluttered a white-gloved hand behind her and snapped up the money as quick as a blink. Then she requested Mister Gosling to insert the boy into the shop only after she and Miranda had gone inside, as she did not wish to be publicly associated with him.

'Come, child!' she said to Miranda, and swept into the shop to the delicate tinkling of a bell. Mister Gosling was about to push Barnacle after when he was forestalled. Miranda, ever eager with a hook, caught Barnacle round the neck with the handle of her parasol and jerked him through the door. Mister Gosling laughed, waved, and went back to the *Lady of the Lea*.

Inside the shop, Barnacle, quite overcome by the marvellous McDippers, rubbed his neck and retired into the obscurity of Mister Levy's stock, so that, apart from his head, hands and feet, he might have been just another waistcoat among thousands.

'Ah! Mrs McDipper and Miss Miranda! What an honour! What a pleasure!' Mister Levy, trotting out of nowhere, came at his customers with a fluttering, anxious manner, like a Hebrew moth in a church. He was a beaming little man with big ears and a big nose that were all connected together by gold-rimmed spectacles. 'I was only saying to Mrs Levy this morning that it's a long time since we've seen Mrs McDipper!'

'And how is Mrs Levy?' inquired Mrs McDipper graciously. 'Ay trust she enjoys good health, Mister Levy?'

As she spoke she moved towards a tailor's dummy that was attired in a splendid blue uniform, rich with gold braid, such as Lord Nelson might have worn for his funeral. She sighed and fondly patted its shoulder.

'Ah! Still the pride of my house, Mrs McDipper!' said Mister Levy gently. 'Only yesterday I was offered ten pound, but I said no. It's a sacred trust. But what can I do for you? Or is it something for Miss Miranda? A cape, perhaps?'

Before Mrs McDipper could stop him, he was behind his counter and rummaging away like a portly terrier. Suddenly he gave a cry of triumph.

'Ah! Here it is! Look, look! So smart! It might have been made for Miss Miranda!' He held up a furry article, peculiar, like half a black cheese. 'Real Russian sable!'

Miranda's eyes glittered with desire. Helplessly she held out a hand. Mrs McDipper slapped it down.

'Russian sable?' she marvelled. 'Wapping rat more like it! But I've not come for meself or for me daughter, Mister Levy. I've come about – about –' She peered round the shop until she spied Mister Gosling's waistcoat huddled among its friends. 'About him. I want you to do what you can, Mister Levy, with that boy. But not a penny more than five shillings.'

Mister Levy looked at Barnacle. He put his head on one side as if to improve the view. He sighed and murmured, 'Five shillings,' very doubtfully. He shook his head again and put away the cape. Miranda's eyes followed it like hungry mice.

'Perhaps if you would step into the stockroom, dear lady,' suggested Mister Levy, 'and show me what you have in mind?'

Mrs McDipper looked at him thoughtfully. He returned her gaze unblinkingly.

'Very well, Mister Levy,' she said at length, and, instructing her daughter to keep an eye on Barnacle, she followed Mister Levy through a doorway behind the counter.

Miranda watched after her carefully; then she sighed and went up to the tailor's dummy. She stroked its lapel and fondly took it by the sleeve. Wonderingly, Barnacle approached. She looked at him. Her eyes were wistful and dreamy.

'My pa,' she murmured. 'Captain McDipper. It's what he was wearing when he was took.'

'Cor!' breathed Barnacle, awed beyond measure by the glory that had once been Captain McDipper. He spied a small round hole just above where the Captain's sweetbread would have been. He touched it respectfully. 'Shot, were 'e?'

'Moth.'

'Your ma clock 'im one, then, wiv 'er fryin' pan?'

Miranda shook her head. 'He fell overboard and drowned.'

'Windy, were it?'

'No. He was overcome. Took poorly. Soused to the eyeballs.'

'Oh. Gin?'

'Rum. Poor old pa.'

Sadly she let go of the Captain's sleeve, which, as if from force of habit, remained for a moment, convivially raised, before it fell, empty. Barnacle felt curiously moved, not so much by the tragic end of Captain McDipper as by Miranda's memories and feelings for all that was left of him. They made him feel lonely and envious. He fumbled in his trousers.

'I got a dead 'un too,' he said, fishing out the locket and the spoon that was tangled in the chain. Quickly he hid the spoon in Mister Gosling's waistcoat and, opening the locket, displayed the tiny picture within. 'Me ma,' he said proudly. 'That's me an' 'er when I was little.'

Miranda stared at it. She laughed. 'What do you take me for! That's a church picture! You nicked it, didn't you?'

Indignantly Barnacle denied the charge and was about to explain how his ma had hung the locket round his neck just before she popped her clogs, when Mrs McDipper and Mister Levy came back. Hastily he stowed the locket away.

The visit to the stockroom turned out to have been a wonderful success. Mister Levy was full of admiration. Mrs McDipper had found exactly the right garments for the young gentleman. What an eye Mrs McDipper had! It never ceased to amaze Mister Levy. And Mrs Levy, too. They often talked about it. Only the other day Mrs Levy had said, 'Mister Levy, I've never known such an eye for quality as Mrs McDipper's!'

Now, if the young gentleman would step this way, urged Mister Levy, his spectacles gleaming with honest pleasure at the thought of what was in store, and try the garments on, he would see for himself how smartly he had been suited. He beckoned, and Barnacle, after an inquiring look at Mrs McDipper, followed him through the dark doorway and into the dense forest of hanging garments that was Mister Levy's stockroom.

Mrs McDipper's selection lay over the chair: a brown jacket, a grey shirt, check trousers, a waistcoat of mustard-pot yellow and a pair of black boots. A complete boy, so to speak, lacking only noise and appetite. There was a hat, too, that Mister Levy said he was prepared to throw in; but Barnacle was so overcome by the waistcoat, which had brass buttons almost as big as half-crowns, that he scarcely heard. He picked it up . . .

The shop bell rang. Mister Levy fluttered anxiously. He was sorry to have to leave the young man to put the garments on by himself, but please to do so and not to worry if the fit wasn't quite perfect, as Mrs Levy was a real genius with alterations and ought to have been in Savile Row. Then he trotted back into the shop.

It was a customer, a tall, thin gentleman with a patch over one eye, a crutch under one arm, and a neatly darned trouser over one leg. The other leg wasn't there. In its place was a varnished wooden peg. Mister Levy's heart sank. It was Mister Jelks. But Mister Levy was a shopkeeper and Mister Jelks was a customer.

'Why, if it isn't Mister Jelks!' he cried warmly. 'I was only saying to Mrs Levy last night that it's a long time since we've seen Mister Jelks!'

'My respects to your good lady, Levy,' returned Mister Jelks gruffly. 'Anything for me today?'

Mister Levy looked uncomfortable. 'Not exactly, Mister Jelks, not exactly what you have in mind. To be honest with you,' he confessed, 'single-legged garments are hard to come by these days.'

Mister Jelks shrugged his free shoulder. 'Keep trying, Levy, that's all I ask.'

'Now why not take a two-legged pair?' urged Mister Levy, almost pleadingly. 'I can make you a special price. Take a two-legged pair and just cut off the other leg. Mrs Levy will –'

'As I've told you before and as I tell you again,' interruped Mister Jelks, 'I ain't paying for what I can't use. So keep trying, Levy, keep trying.'

He was about to leave when his solitary eye fell upon the resplendent tailor's dummy. He jerked and thumped towards it.

'I'm afraid it's not for sale, Mister Jelks,' murmured Mister Levy, with an unhappy glance at Mrs McDipper. 'It's in the nature of a trust.'

'It was may late husband,' explained the widow, with melancholy dignity. 'Captain McDipper, you know.'

'Sorry to hear it, ma'am,' grunted Mister Jelks. 'My condolences. But better to lose a husband than a leg. You can always get yourself another.'

Mrs McDipper clutched at her bosom and went very red.

'You're blushing, ma!' said Miranda, needlessly.

Mister Jelks glanced at her sharply. 'If she was mine, ma'am,' he said to her mother, 'I'd put her across my knee.'

Then he jerked and thumped towards the door. Mister Levy hastened to open it for him. Mister Jelks acknowledged the courtesy with a nod. 'Keep on trying, Levy, keep on trying,' he reminded the shopkeeper, and hobbled out into the street.

'A hard man,' sighed Mister Levy, shutting the door, 'a very hard man to please.'

Mister Jelks was the bane of his life. He was an aggravation and a nagging reproach. He was the one customer in all the world that the Nautical Outfitter always failed to fit. Mrs McDipper didn't like him either. His advice about getting herself another husband, in the presence of her self-righteous daughter and in front of the late Captain himself, had made her conspicuous. She felt angry and ashamed.

'Barnacle!' she shouted, seeking distraction. 'Barnacle! Oh, where the devil is that boy?'

'Why don't you open your eyes, ma?' inquired Miranda. 'What do you think that is?'

A brown jacket, a yellow waistcoat and check trousers had been standing for some time by the counter, underneath a horrible tweed cap. The garments were quite motionless, and standing apparently of their own accord. It was uncanny . . .

'So smart he looks!' cried Mister Levy admiringly. 'Beautiful, beautiful!'

Mrs McDipper stared. 'Are you in there, Barnacle?'

'Yus, missus,' came the muffled reply. 'I been 'ere all the time.'

Mrs McDipper frowned. She shook her head.

'Such style!' marvelled Mister Levy, gazing raptly at his stock. 'The shoulders . . . the hang of the trousers . . . You wouldn't know him!'

'That's because you can't see him, Mister Levy!' said Mrs McDipper, still failing to detect any sign of Mister Gosling's boy.

'But that's the way they're wearing them these days, dear lady! Go down Bond Street and you'd be surprised!'

Mrs McDipper didn't doubt it, but what was suitable for Bond Street wasn't right for a barge. The garments would have to be taken up and taken in. Or there would be no sale.

'Very well, dear lady,' sighed Mister Levy. 'Mrs Levy will attend to it right away.' Ordinarily he would have argued and then insisted on three days for the alterations, but his failure over Mister Jelks still rankled, and he was determined not to fail again.

'And that cap, Mister Levy –'

'I was throwing it in for the same money –'

'Better throw it out, then! Let him have the midshipman's hat. And remember, Mister Levy, not a penny more than five shillings.'

'Not a penny more, Mrs McDipper. Just like we agreed.'

He stared at her, and she stared back. Faintly, almost invisibly, he twitched an eye; and Mrs McDipper, even more invisibly, did likewise. Then Mister Levy fluttered his hands like a conjuror and the standing garments moved and trudged after him through the dark doorway, to be taken up and taken in by Mrs Levy.

For a moment there was silence in the shop; then Miranda said: 'I saw that, ma.'

'Saw what, miss?'

'You winking.'

Mrs McDipper protested that she'd done no such thing and it had been something in her eye. Miranda said, yes, and she'd a good idea what, and her ma ought to be ashamed. Only five shillings indeed, when anybody could see that them clothes must have cost an enormous amount more, and she'd half a mind to tell Uncle Tom!

Mrs McDipper lost her temper and threatened to follow Mister Jelks's advice and lay her daughter across her knee, and anyway what business was it of Miranda's if her mother chose to oblige Mister Gosling with an extra shilling or two without his knowing? After all, how could you expect a lazy loafer like Tom Gosling to put by enough money to buy his barge and raise himself to Mrs McDipper's level without a little help from a friend?

She paused for breath. Miranda was staring at her oddly. Mrs McDipper fidgeted and felt like crying. How stern and unforgiving were the young, and how little they cared about the feelings of grown-up people! Mrs McDipper almost wished that Miranda herself would fall victim to an unsuitable attachment so at least her mother could get her own back . . .

'Poor old ma!' said Miranda. Then, as if a thought had just struck her, she lifted her parasol and fondly touched the late Captain McDipper on either shoulder, as if elevating him to a ghostly knighthood. 'Uncle Tom ain't bad,' she conceded, 'but you could do better, ma, if you put your mind to it.'

'I'm sure we could all do better than we're doing,' said Mrs McDipper, 'if we put our minds to it, miss!'

Miranda shrugged her shoulders. 'Anyway, you didn't have to buy up half the shop for that boy!' She paused as her wandering gaze lighted upon the counter behind which Mister Levy had put away the sable cape. Her eyes grew wistful, and she went on reproachfully, 'Especially when your own flesh and blood has to go without. Really, ma, anybody would have thought it was Barnacle's birthday!'

ELEVEN

Everything is of interest to the interesting man. Inspector Creaker, still wearing his heavy caped coat and his high-crowned black hat, stood in a doorway that obliged him with its shadow, thoughtfully observing the afternoon's activity on Broken Wharf. In particular his attention was drawn towards the half-dozen men who were shovelling natural merchandise from hand-carts into sacks and loading them on to the *Lady of the Lea*. Presently he raised a gloved hand and placed it firmly on the shoulder of a fidgeting black shadow beside him. The shadow jumped.

'Is that the man, Mister Roberts?' murmured the Inspector.

The master sweep blinked and peered in the direction the Inspector had indicated. He still hadn't got over his fright at finding the Inspector waiting for him again in Newport Court; and, although it had turned out that he was only wanted to go and identify somebody, he couldn't suppress his stupid fear that, at any moment, the Inspector would change his mind and ask to see his birth certificate. The Inspector's fingers tightened on his shoulder.

'Well, Mister Roberts?'

Mister Roberts looked hard at the shirt-sleeved individual standing on the deck of the barge. He nodded vigorously. Yes. That was the dirty great ruffian he'd come up against outside of the Jolly Bargeman. No doubt about it. Look there! You could even see the mark of a boy's bite on his arm! It was the very bite that had been bleeding outside of the Jolly Bargeman, which, Mister Roberts would have taken his Bible oath on it, had been done by his little animal of a boy. He'd have known them tooth marks anywhere!

'Thank you, Mister Roberts. I'm obliged to you.'

'Then – then can I go now, sir?'

'Just one thing more, Mister Roberts . . .' Mister Roberts's blood froze. The Inspector went on: 'Is that him? Is that your boy, Mister Roberts? Is that Absalom Brown?'

Mister Roberts looked. Along the wharf, followed by a duchess and her girl, stalked a sawn-off little gent in brown and checks, with a gorgeous weskit and a face as proud as sixpence. Mister Roberts gave way to a small howl of derision.

'What, *'im*? That there toffed-up gent me little animal? You must be jokin', Mr Inspector! Mine were as black as yer 'at!'

'Are you sure of that?'

Mister Roberts opened his mouth. The Inspector raised a warning hand. 'No. Not on your Bible oath, Mister Roberts, just in case you might be perjuring yourself. You can go now.'

The master sweep heaved a sigh of relief and hobbled away, as foolishly thankful as he had been foolishly afraid. The Inspector remained in the doorway, still watching. Everything was of interest to the interesting man . . .

The man on the barge, known to the Inspector as Mister Tom Gosling, had dropped the sack he had been heaving so that some of its contents had spilled out on to the deck. He was staring at the approaching boy. He was amazed. He shook his head. He rubbed his eyes and looked again. He put his hands on his hips and laughed aloud, unbelievingly.

'No!' he cried. 'It can't be! It ain't possible! It's not the same boy!'

The Inspector nodded thoughtfully. His continuing interest

had been rewarded. When the boy's old master had denied him, the Inspector had been doubtful; but now that the new one had denied him, the Inspector doubted no longer. In his book of grammar, two negatives made a positive as surely as night followed day. The boy was the boy he had been looking for. He was the boy whose birthdays were to be stopped. All that remained was to be sure that the locket was still in his possession. The Inspector waited . . .

'You've done wonders, Mrs McDipper!' cried Mister Gosling, still unable to believe that the fashionable individual who stood before him, polishing his brass buttons on his sleeve and fiddling with his midshipman's hat, was really his skinny little Barnacle.

' 'Ere's yer weskit back, mister,' said Barnacle, holding out the shabby article somewhat distastefully. He was immensely lifted by his reception, and felt that not to be recognized as himself was the highest honour that could have been bestowed on him.

'And – and all for five shillings?' marvelled Mister Gosling, turning to Mrs McDipper, who was beaming with pleasure over the success of her choice. 'Including the hat?'

'Five shillings, Mister Gosling? What do you take me for? I don't go throwing other people's money about like confetti! Three shillings was all I spent! On me solemn honour it was,' she promised, crossing her fingers behind her back. 'You've got two shillings change, Mister Gosling, two shillings to put back in your moneybox!'

Miranda's eyes popped like they'd fall out. 'Ma!' she began, shrill as pins and needles, then she said, 'Ow!' as Mrs McDipper's shiny boot with silver laces shot out like black lightning and caught her on the ankle. She screwed up her eyes, and when she opened them again there was a nasty light in them. 'I was just thinking, ma,' she said, and stopped.

'Oh? And what were you thinking, miss?'

'I was just thinking about Mister Levy's sable cape. I was wondering if you were going to buy it for me, ma.'

Mrs McDipper opened and shut her fist as if she wished she'd got her frying pan in it. Then she said, very quiet-like, 'I told you dear, it wasn't sable. It was *rat*!' She came down on 'rat' somewhat heavy.

'But I liked it, ma.'

'I'll get you some real Russian sable, dear,' said Mrs McDipper, after thinking it over, 'one day.'

'When, ma?'

'Oh . . . oh . . . next week, then. When the *December Rose* comes in.'

'The *December Rose*?'

Barnacle looked up from admiring the way his trousers ended in boots. 'What's that?'

The words had stirred in his memory, and he grew cold inside his new clothes. *December Rose . . . December Rose . . .* He was in the dark again, listening to Smooth-and-Bony, and to Fat-Guts, and, worst of all, to Whistling Edge . . .

'It's a ship, Barnacle,' Mister Gosling was saying. 'It's a ship that comes over from Hamburg every month. Why do you want to know?'

'Dunno, mister,' mumbled Barnacle, fixing his gaze on Mister Gosling's bare feet as if they were the most interesting articles in the world. He didn't want to look up. He was suddenly frightened that the big man would guess the truth from his eyes and know that he'd heard of the *December Rose* in the house where he'd nicked the locket, and that would be the end of everything. 'It's just that it were such a queer name,' he said, shifting his gaze from Mister Gosling's feet as if his very toes had eyes.

He noticed the spillage from the sack Mister Gosling had been heaving. He sniffed. He frowned. He looked at the sacks that were already piled up on the deck. He sniffed again, and a terrible suspicion entered his mind. 'What's in them sacks, mister?'

Miranda made a sniggering noise. 'It's horse –' she began.

'– manure!' finished up Mrs McDipper quickly.

Barnacle investigated one of the sacks. He recoiled, outraged. 'No, it ain't. It's 'orse shit! That's what it is. It's bleedin' 'orse shit!'

Mrs McDipper went red. She told Miranda to stop up her ears. She wasn't having any daughter of hers listening to such language.

'What are you loadin' up wiv that for, mister?' pursued Barnacle, feeling indignant about the *Lady*'s cargo. What was the use of being dressed up proper if you ended up sailing with shit?

'We take it downriver and sell it to the farms, Barnacle,' explained Mister Gosling. 'It helps things to grow. And then we bring back hay for the horses so that they can make more of it. See?'

Barnacle brooded. Then his face brightened. He had thought of something. 'It's clever, mister,' he conceded. 'It's clever all right. I got to 'and it to you. So we makes money out o' both ends of a 'orse.'

Mister Gosling laughed, and even Mrs McDipper looked as if she was in danger of doing the same.

'Come along, Miranda,' she said, turning away her face. 'Come and change out of them good clothes.'

'In a minute, ma.'

Mrs McDipper didn't argue. She asked Mister Gosling if he could spare a moment so that she could give him back his two shillings, and waited for him to follow her off the barge.

'Barnacle,' murmured Miranda, smiling and coming close as soon as her mother had gone.

'Yus, miss?'

'That locket you've got . . .'

'What about it, miss?'
'Show us it again.'
'Why?'
'Oh, I just wanted to see. It was pretty . . .'
Barnacle beamed. Praise for his property was praise for him. He fumbled for the locket. Then he stopped. He felt peculiar. He'd had a sudden sensation of being watched. He stared across at the men working on the wharf. None of them seemed to be looking his way. Then he noticed a deep doorway in one of the warehouses, like a black mouth. He thought he saw a shadowy figure in it, and the faint glitter of watchful eyes. Then there was a clatter of hooves and a grinding of wheels and a tall cart rumbled between him and the doorway and stopped, shutting off the view.
'Come on,' urged Miranda. 'Let's see it.'
Reluctantly Barnacle took out the locket. Miranda gazed at it with shining interest. Gently she took it from him and held it up to her neck.
'Are they real jewels?' she asked, pointing to the bright little stones that surrounded the enamelled black eagle.
'Dunno, miss.'
'If they are, it'll be worth some money.'
' 'Ow much?'
'Oh, five or six pounds. Maybe more, even . . .'
'Cor!' breathed Barnacle, suddenly overcome by an avarice beyond the reach of his dreams. 'Let's 'ave it back, miss!'
'What do you want it for?' asked Miranda, opening and shutting her eyes like coppers' lamps. 'It looks much better on a girl!'
'Like I told yer, it's me ma an' me when I was little. Let's 'ave it back!'
'Oh, take it, then!' cried Miranda angrily, almost throwing the locket back. 'And I hope it brings you bad luck!'
As he took it and thrust it into his jacket, the tall cart on the

wharf moved away. The dark doorway was empty; the shadowy figure had gone. Barnacle felt curiously relieved. Again he stared across the wharf, but he saw only men working, and none of them was interested in him. The only new arrival was a portly, red-faced man in a stripy suit with a brown hat on the back of his head. He was leaning against a wall not far from the doorway; but far from watching Barnacle, he was studiously peeling an apple with a bright, sharp knife.

TWELVE

'When a person's been fitted out from top to bottom by Mister Solomon Levy,' explained Miranda, sitting on a barrel and swinging her legs, one afternoon after unloading, 'at enormous expense, a person must expect to be looked at more than when a person went about half-naked in rags.'

Barnacle shook his head. 'Not looked at, miss. Watched.'

'Oh, looked at, watched, stared at! What's the difference?' cried Miranda impatiently. 'You ought to be grateful to be taken such notice of, else me and ma and Mister Levy just wasted our time and money!'

Barnacle sighed. She was right, of course. When you'd been done over by Mrs Levy, with her fingers full of needles and her mouth full of pins, it was only natural that you should be an object of interest. You were something worth looking at. But being watched was different. When you were being looked at, you could see the eyes what was doing it, but when you was being watched, you could only feel them.

It was a tickling, prickling feeling and he'd had it, on and off, ever since Friday, when he'd come back from Mister Levy's. At first, he'd wondered if it was his shirt itching, but he got it higher up than that, in the back of his neck. Most often it happened at Broken Wharf, but once or twice he'd felt it downriver, in the Traveller's Rest; and even at night, when he was safe in his bunk and peering privately at the valuable, 'me an' me ma', he felt that eyes were trying to crawl through the wooden sides of the *Lady* and get at him. The only times he really felt free and easy were when the *Lady* was in mid-river, sailing through sunshine and fog.

'Beautiful, ain't she?' Mister Gosling would call out, with a tremendous wave of his arm.

' 'Oo? 'Er wiv the fryin' pan, mister?'

'I meant the *Lady*, Barnacle, the *Lady of the Lea*! Not that Mrs McDipper ain't beautiful too!'

'I see what yer means, mister!' Barnacle shouted back, and pointed to the bosomy great sprit-sail and the little red mizzen that billowed and wagged behind. 'Just like 'er wiv the fryin' pan an' 'er wiv the 'ook!'

Mister Gosling laughed and threatened that he'd tell the ladies, but he never did; so the mid-river times were happy, even though the cargo steamed and stank.

'I think he fancies me,' said Miranda suddenly, and stopped swinging her legs.

' 'Oo, miss?'

He felt that there were insects crawling up his neck. He turned . . .

'He's gone now,' said Miranda. 'I think your ugly face must have frightened him off.'

As usual, there was nothing to be seen. The dark doorway was empty; three or four men were playing cards on a barrel top, and an out-of-work youth, with his hands in his pockets and hay-coloured hair, was whistling, *'Oh dear, what can the matter be? . . . Oh dear, what can the matter be?'*, and a dog was barking at nothing . . .

Barnacle concluded that, somehow or other, it must have been his shirt that had been prickling the back of his neck . . .

On the morning of Saturday the twenty-third, at twenty-five

minutes past nine by Aldgate Church clock, and half past by his own steel watch, Inspector Creaker left his lodgings in Dock Street and once more walked briskly towards the City. This time, however, his destination was not Mr Hastymite's club, but a cab-stand near St Paul's. He hired a cab, and, giving an address in a fashionable square just off Pall Mall, settled back inside to enjoy the comfort of leather and privacy, which was a comfort he could seldom afford.

When the cab arrived, he paid the driver with money he had carefully counted out during the journey, and stepped down on to the pavement, where he stood for a few moments, as if his sole purpose in coming had been to admire the imposing front of his lordship's London house.

He noted, partly with approval and partly with a curious feeling of disquiet, that the smashed window had been skilfully repaired, so that no sign remained of the escape of Absalom Brown. He wished that the glazier could have performed a similar miracle upon himself, for the recollection still let the cold into his heart.

He mounted the steps, knocked and, while he waited, bent down to brush away some invisible dust from his boots. The door was opened and he was admitted, without delay, into his lordship's presence.

Mr Hastymite was present and so was her ladyship, with her usual little smile, and her usual little laugh, and her usual remark about leaving the gentlemen to discuss their affairs of State.

'Now promise me, Mr Hastymite,' she said, as she rustled to the door, 'that when our new place in the country is finished, you will come and be our very first guest.'

Mr Hastymite, who was standing by the window, bowed and said he would be honoured, and that he looked forward very much to visiting what, he had heard, was to be one of the finest houses in Hertfordshire. Her ladyship laughed and left the room.

'I would offer you a glass of sherry, Inspector,' said his lordship, an immense, mountainous Minister of State who dwarfed the chair he sat in, 'but I fancy that ale would be more to your taste, eh, eh?'

Without waiting for a reply, he rang for a servant, and, while the ale was being brought, the Inspector observed how completely the room had been restored to order. The walls, where the terror of Absalom Brown had marked them, had been repapered; the smashed ornaments had been replaced; and even the oriental rug in front of the fireplace, where the boy had crouched, glaring like a wild animal, had been changed. It was as if the boy, whose birthdays were to be stopped, had never been born.

'And now, man,' said his lordship, after the Inspector, seated rigidly in a chair, had been supplied with ale, 'what have you to report?'

The Inspector consulted his notebook. The *December Rose* had been sighted in the Estuary and would be lying off Gravesend by late afternoon. However, the fog –

'I don't want a weather report, Inspector!' snapped his lordship. 'What about the locket . . . and the boy? Have you done your duty, eh, eh?'

'The boy has been found, your lordship.'

'And – and –?'

'He is being watched, closely watched.'

'Watched?' His lordship leaned forward sharply. 'What the devil do you mean, man? Why haven't you acted? Or do you mean to let that boy escape you for a second time, eh, eh?'

The Inspector, staring straight ahead of him, said almost in a whisper that the boy would not escape him, but before he could act he needed to be absolutely sure that the locket was in the boy's possession. So far he had been unable to –

'But this is intolerable!' raged the great Minister, his huge shape shaking with anger. 'That – that a little animal should hold in his filthy hands the – the –'

'The security of the State,' put in Mr Hastymite quickly. He spoke, as always, very softly, and his voice had the effect of calming his lordship down. 'But tell his lordship,' he went on, while the Minister busied himself with lighting a cigar, 'what arrangements you have made if, by any chance, the boy should escape you again. There is so little time . . .'

The Inspector, addressing his boots, explained that the *December Rose* would be watched and as soon as the messenger, Colonel Brodsky, came ashore, he would be seized –

'But the funds, man, the funds!' suddenly shouted the Minister, who was famous for his fiery patriotism; and indeed, as he puffed furiously at his cigar, there was something volcanic about the blue smoke that came out of him.

'His lordship means,' murmured Mr Hastymite, 'that the funds must never be available to those violent men for their wicked purposes. The money, Inspector, is more important to us than the man.'

'Yes, sir. I understand that.'

'Do you, Inspector?' inquired his lordship coldly. 'I am beginning to doubt it. It seems to me that you are taking this matter altogether too lightly. Perhaps if the money had been going into your own pocket instead of into Her Majesty's Treasury, you would have been a little sharper about your duty, eh, eh?'

'That is not so, m'lord,' returned the Inspector quietly, and was surprised at the steadiness of his own voice as he contradicted the great Minister. 'I am paid enough for my needs.'

'Enough to afford to come here in a cab, Inspector, eh, eh?'

'I came by cab, m'lord, so as not to be observed.'

'The Inspector was quite right,' said Mr Hastymite, coming away from the window. 'We all know that secrecy must be maintained.'

'Not long ago, m'lord,' went on the Inspector, 'there was a man, a fellow with a crooked nose and a scar on his face, who seemed to be taking quite an interest in me. I received the impression that he would have been very pleased to discover who my superiors were. And I need hardly tell you, m'lord, for what terrible purpose.'

The Minister scowled. He was not a coward, but he understood that his security and the security of the State were one and the same, He was, as he remembered the *Morning Post* had once pointed out, the very spirit of Old England . . .

'Very well, Inspector,' he muttered, examining his smouldering cigar. 'But I warn you, I will not tolerate another failure. The boy –'

'– will not escape, m'lord,' said the Inspector. 'He is being watched, closely watched.'

'Your men? They are sharp fellows, eh, eh?'

The Inspector signified that his men were indeed sharp, and that the man who was, at this very moment, observing the boy was one of the sharpest in the Force. He was a man who could appear and disappear remarkably; he was a man not to be shaken off; and he was a man who, as soon as he clapped eyes on the locket, would –

'– put a stop to the boy's birthdays, eh, Inspector?' smiled Mr Hastymite. 'I believe that was the expression you used.'

'No, sir,' said the Inspector. 'It was the expression *you* used.'

'Was it? Oh well, never mind. We all know what it means.'

THIRTEEN

Of all the flowers in the garden of the Roebuck at Richmond, of all the ornamental bushes, quick and twittering with yellow-breasted bluetits, none was more flowery and ornamental than Mrs McDipper and her daughter, Miranda.

'I told you, ma,' said Miranda, looking round at their bee-haunted rivals, 'not to wear that hat. It looks just like one of them bushes.'

'I'll ask you to keep a civil tongue in your head, miss,' warned her mother. 'Else there'll be no sables for you off the *December Rose* tonight.'

The McDippers and their neighbours, Tom Gosling and his boy, were in holiday mood, as they sat taking tea in the riverside garden of the inn. Though it was only Saturday afternoon, Mister Gosling was dressed up for Sunday, with his hair as shiny as a hat. He looked as smart as an alderman, and nobody would know, to look at him, that he didn't own his own barge.

All in all, theirs was as handsome a table as any of the dozen round about, and, try as he might, Barnacle could not see a single waistcoat that rivalled in splendour his own mustard-pot garment with its buttons like gold half-crowns. So it was only natural they should be looked at and winked at, even by the beady-eyed waiters who kept hopping among the tables like crows in dirty aprons, picking up money and crumbs.

'I see'd 'im before!' said Barnacle, with interest.

'Who?'

' 'Im over there.'

'Don't point!' said Mrs McDipper. 'It's common. It makes you look so conspicuous.'

Barnacle mumbled into his piece of cake that, if he didn't point, how was anybody to know who he was pointing at? He shrugged his shoulders.

The gent he'd aimed his finger at was sitting at a table by himself. He was a cheerful-looking gent with a red face and his hat on the back of his head. He was wearing a stripy suit and was peeling an apple like he wanted to get a confession out of it. He had one of them folding pocket-knives with about a hundred blades: some for apples, some for pears, some for boys, and little ones for babies, thought Barnacle humorously . . .

'Children!' Mrs McDipper was saying, frowning at a nearby family being plagued by little shriekers in the sun. 'More trouble than they're worth,' she sighed, glancing at her own daughter and at Barnacle. 'But I expect you're finding that out for yourself, Mister Gosling.'

'Oh, I don't know,' said he. 'When all's said and done, Mrs McDipper, they're company on dark nights. And,' he smiled at Barnacle, 'now I've got used to him, I don't think I'd change my little Barnacle for all the tea in China!'

Barnacle felt enormously pleased, even though he thought, privately, that Mister Gosling would have been a fool to pass up such a bargain.

'Talking of tea,' said Mrs McDipper, fumbling in her bag and producing a small silver flask, 'will you take a drop of rum in your beverage, Mister Gosling? Captain McDipper would never touch it without rum. He always said that tea's like a dog's nose. You just don't know where it's been. Rum, he said, was the only thing to kill the germs.'

'Just a drop, then,' said Mister Gosling, offering his cup. 'What was good enough for the Captain is more than good enough for me.'

He looked at her very earnestly as she dispensed the rum; but she avoided his eyes, and, as she put away the flask, murmured half to herself: 'Ah, he was the best of men, the very best! I can still see him, standing up there on deck, like a lord of the river!'

Her eyes grew misty with memories; and Barnacle, to whom the Captain was no more than a disembodied suit, had a sudden vision of it, bolt-upright on the barge, with Mrs McDipper twined fondly round one trouser leg and Miranda round the other, and mother and daughter gazing rapturously up at the Captain's empty collar.

'But it must be all of ten years since you lost him,' said Mister Gosling. 'Surely it's about time that –'

'You know my feelings, Tom Gosling,' interposed Mrs McDipper gently. 'I'll always be true to his wishes. Clara, he said to me, if ever I should be taken from you, don't throw yourself away. You're a fine woman, Clara, and you'll own your own barge. So, for my sake, Clara, wed a man of substance, a man of property . . .'

'Cor!' breathed Barnacle, and rubbed his eyes. He had just seen, in his mind's eye, a wonderful sight. He had just seen the Captain's suit with his Mister Gosling inside of it and looking a treat. 'Cor!' he breathed again, but this time a little sadly as his vision faded and there was Mister Gosling, sitting at the table and looking no better than himself. Then Barnacle had an idea . . .

He looked round. The cheerful gent was minding his own business and working away at his apple. His knife kept flashing as the sunshine caught it, and a coil of red peel was dripping down like blood. There was an old tree in the corner of the garden nearest the river. It was huge and thick and leafy, with loving hearts carved into its trunk and a wooden seat going all the way round . . . as if, when it got tired of standing, there was somewhere for it to sit down.

'That's an interestin' tree, miss,' said Barnacle. 'I never see'd one like that before. All them 'earts! Let's go an' 'ave a look!'

He stood up. Miranda looked at him uneasily. She wondered, fleetingly, if his new clothes had given him ideas above his size and station. She wondered if he had the impudence to fancy her and was aiming to carve another heart. Then, dismissing her fears as groundless, on account of Barnacle's not having a knife, she followed him to the tree.

'Well?' she said, when they stood beneath its branches. She dug her parasol into the earth, folded her hands on its crook, and waited.

'About me locket, miss –'

'What? That old thing? You and your ma when you was little? What about it, then?'

'D'you really think it might be worth somefink, miss?'

'How should I know? I ain't a pawnbroker. Let's have another look at it.'

Barnacle reached into his pocket. He paused, and rubbed the back of his neck. He looked across the garden, and was just in time to catch the cheerful gent smiling at him. He frowned . . .

'I'm waiting,' said Miranda. 'We ain't got all day.'

Barnacle shook his head. 'What's 'e up to now?' he muttered, as the gent, with a roguish wink and a saucy grin, nodded at Miranda and lifted up a long curl of red peel to his neck, as if he was offering either a playful necklace or an elaborately cut throat.

'I think he fancies me,' said Miranda, divining that her peculiar admirer was suggesting that she was worthy of jewels. 'Here! Give us that locket! I'll show him!'

As if he had heard her, her admirer leaned forward, and, putting down the apple peel, picked up a pair of cherries and held them to his ear. His grin was enormous . . .

' 'E looks orf 'is 'ead to me,' said Barnacle. 'Let's go round the other side of the tree, miss.'

Miranda hesitated; then, feeling that the man was making her look ridiculous, pulled up her parasol and stalked after Barnacle round the other side of the tree. They sat down, side by side.

' 'Ere, miss, 'ere it is,' said Barnacle, producing the locket. ' 'Ow much d'you think I'd get for it?'

She took the locket and gazed, with unwilling admiration, at the elegant black eagle and the bright little stones all round it. She weighed it in her hand, then shook her head and gave it back to Barnacle.

'I don't know,' she said. 'Why don't you ask Mister Thompson?'

'Oo's 'e?'

'Pawnshop next door to Levy's.'

'D'you think I'd get eleven pound?'

'If them's real diamonds, you might. You could ask Annie in the Traveller's. She used to work for a pawnbroker once. You'll be seeing her tonight.'

'Will you an' your ma be there, miss?'

'No. It's the *December Rose* tonight. I'll be getting me Russian sables.'

'I wish you well to wear 'em, miss. Mister Thompson, did you say?'

'That's right. Next door to Levy's. But why do you want to sell it? It would look much better on me than on Mister Thompson!'

Barnacle didn't answer. His reasons for wanting to sell the locket were very private. If Mister Gosling valued him above all the tea in China, then the least he could do was to value Mister Gosling above the locket. He was thinking of Captain McDipper's suit and Mister Gosling inside of it. He was thinking of the way that Mister Gosling always looked at Mrs McDipper, and the way that Mrs McDipper might look at Mister Gosling, standing up on deck like a lord of the river . . .

'It's time we were going,' said Miranda, having failed in her second bid for the locket. She stood up and, together with Barnacle, walked back round the tree. They returned to their table in silence. They were both so absorbed in their thoughts – Miranda's of her forthcoming sables, and Barnacle's of getting to the pawnshop – that they never noticed that, under the seat, round the other side from where they'd been sitting, was a long curl of red apple peel.

FOURTEEN

Saturday was Mister Levy's Sunday so even at half past five his shop was shut. But it was just possible to see, by jumping up and down at his window like a flea, that Captain McDipper was still inside. Headless and handless, he stood among the shadows, lording it over the lesser garments and waiting only for a better offer than ten pounds to unwidow his wife.

Next door, however, Saturday was Saturday, and Mister Thompson's best day. His shop was open, and his three brass balls hung in the air like suns that never set.

There was a customer inside, pawning a leather-bound telescope and a marble clock; and Barnacle nibbled and gnawed at his fingernails while Mister Thompson fiddled with the telescope, wound up the clock, consulted his ledger and wrote out the tickets with a pen that kept running dry. He was in a terrible hurry, as Mister Gosling had only gone to the Jolly Bargeman and would be back in half an hour.

At length the transaction was completed and the pawner departed with his money, happy to have exchanged time and distance for here and now. Barnacle approached the counter, which was almost as high as he; and the pawnbroker's pale round face, like the ghost of one of his own brass balls, loomed over him.

'And what can we do for you, my little man?' inquired Mister Thompson, as if there were several Mister Thompsons all inside each other, and Barnacle was small, single and alone.

He felt confused and frightened. Apart from going into a public house for Mister Roberts's beer, it was the first time he had been in a place of business, a place of commercial transactions, on his own. He stood, breathing deeply, while his eyes darted from side to side as if they wished themselves anywhere but in his head. He didn't know how to begin . . .

It was possible that the pawnbroker guessed his customer's state of mind, as he glanced out through his window as if to see if there was someone of a larger size, ready and waiting to come into the shop, if need be, and take matters in hand. He smiled faintly and rubbed the side of his nose.

'Come along, little man,' he said encouragingly. 'Let's see what you've got! Is it the baby's christening mug, or your father's watch?'

'Wotcher gimme for this?' gasped Barnacle, suddenly producing the locket and holding it out in a desperate hand and with a desperate face.

Even as he did so, he regretted it. The pawnbroker looked surprised. He pursed his lips and took the locket. He held it up on its chain and again glanced out of the window, this time frowningly. Barnacle felt sick with panic. His fine clothes weren't enough. Plainly he was too small to be in business. Mister Thompson was thinking that the locket was nicked . . .

'Well, now,' said the pawnbroker, with a sudden kindly smile, 'how much were you wanting for it, my little man?'

' 'Leven pound!' cried Barnacle, hoarsely.

'Eleven pounds, eh? Well, it's a fine-looking article, even though it's a bit old-fashioned. And I see that the chain is broken. A pity. That brings the value down, you know. Hm! Eleven pounds . . .'

'There's a pitcher inside,' said Barnacle, anxious to make

up for the broken chain. 'It's of me an' me ma, when I was little.'

Mister Thompson opened the locket and examined the picture through a jeweller's glass. Then he shut the locket and looked thoughtfully at Barnacle's waistcoat, and murmured: 'Eleven pounds . . . eleven pounds . . .'

Barnacle sighed with relief. He knew that if he'd been in rags, Mister Thompson would never have believed him, but now it was different. You could tell, from the smile on the pawnbroker's face, that he was thinking that beneath so smart a waistcoat there must beat an honest heart!

'Here, my little man!' said Mister Thompson, as a pleasant thought occurred to him. 'Have a look at this while I'm making up my mind if we can do business together!'

He picked up the telescope that the previous customer had pawned, and handed it to the boy. Barnacle took it and put it to his eye.

'The other way round, little man, the other way round! And – and just pull it and push it till you can see everything clear!'

Kindly he helped Barnacle with the instrument, and then, when he was satisfied that the boy was happily absorbed, he returned to examining the locket, moving nearer to his window for a better light.

Barnacle poked his long eye this way and that, and finally towards the window and up at the sky. He jumped. He'd just seen a chimney-pot, near enough to touch, but almost immediately it was swept away in a rushing river of windows and bricks. He saw a front door and some railings, and he couldn't help marvelling over how interesting everything looked when you saw it like a bright picture in the dark. He shifted so he could see more.

He saw a black-and-white cat on a doorstep, washing its face; and he watched it as if nobody in the whole world had ever seen such a thing before. Suddenly it stopped. Its eyes widened, and it fled. What had frightened it? A dog, maybe? No. A pair of shiny brown boots. They had come to a halt just beside the step. Brown boots and stripy trousers. And higher up, poking out of stripy sleeves, a pair of fat white hands. They were busy. In one was a bright red apple, and in the other, getting ready to peel it, was a folding pocket-knife with a hundred blades!

Silently, Barnacle lowered the telescope. He looked at Mister Thompson. Mister Thompson was looking out of the window. He was looking straight at the man with the knife. He was holding up the locket in one hand and with the other he was pointing at Barnacle, as if to say: HE'S HERE!

Barnacle screamed. He sprang like a little wild animal at the man who'd trapped him and smashed down the telescope as hard as he could on the pawnbroker's arm. He snatched the locket as it was dropped, and rushed wildly out of the shop.

He was too late! The man must have seen what had happened, and he was coming towards Barnacle with his arms spread wide. He'd dropped the apple but he was still holding the knife; and the blade that was ready was the blade for boys.

Barnacle shrieked and turned. Mister Thompson had come out of his shop. He was armed! Enraged by the savage attack on him, he'd snatched up a rusty old cutlass from stock. He was waving it and shouting, and everywhere people were running and rushing and filling up the street.

There was no escape. He could only go back from where he'd come. He fled through Mister Thompson's open door, through the shop and into the parlour at the back. The door on to the yard stood open, as the day was warm, but the walls beyond were too high to climb. But there was a fireplace, a deep, black fireplace; and never did a climbing boy bolt up a chimney with such willingness, such eagerness, such amazing, eye-blinking rapidity, as did Barnacle!

Although the pawnbroker and the watcher with the knife

were no more than seconds behind, by the time they got into the parlour, the boy was gone. They rushed out into the yard. They searched it. They came back and searched the parlour, and then the shop, in case the boy had hidden somewhere under the counter. Then they went back into the yard and concluded that, although it seemed scarcely possible, somehow or other the boy must have got away over the wall. Barnacle heard them. He was a yard and a half up the chimney, clinging on to the brickwork with every scrap of his amazing powers, and not daring to move for fear of dislodging some tell-tale soot.

The shadows on Broken Wharf were deepening, and the tide was almost on the turn. The McDippers had sailed already, but the *Lady*, loaded and ready, still muttered at her moorings like a jilted bride.

'Don't look like your lad's coming, mister,' said the out-of-work youth with hay-coloured hair. 'So how's about taking on a Jack-at-a-Pinch? I can do with the money, I can tell you!'

'No, no,' muttered Mister Gosling. 'I'll give him another quarter of an hour.'

Though he tried not to show it, he was horribly frightened that something had happened to his boy. Mrs McDipper, meaning for the best, had told him that he was a fool to expect gratitude from a child, and that Barnacle, who was as vain as a peacock in his finery, had most likely run away to better himself. But Mister Gosling couldn't believe it.

'Suit yourself, mister,' said the youth, and, thrusting his hands into his pockets, sauntered away, whistling, *'Oh dear, what can the matter be? Oh dear, what can the matter be? Johnny's so long at the fair!'*

Mister Gosling nodded gloomily. The song chimed in too well with his thoughts. 'Oh dear, what can the matter be?' he whispered. 'Barnacle's so long at the –'

He stopped. He listened. Suddenly his heart lifted and he could have wept with relief! He heard the rattle of small feet pelting over the cobbles, and a famous voice screeching wildly: 'Mister! Mister! I'm 'ere!'

A moment later Barnacle appeared. Mister Gosling stared at him. He glared at him in stark disbelief.

'It's me, mister,' said Barnacle.

'I know it's you, Barnacle,' said Mister Gosling, struggling to keep his temper. *'But what the devil have you done to yourself, lad?'*

The watcher with the knife had not given up. He felt in his bones that the boy had not gone far. He searched the streets and doorways round the pawnbroker's over and over again. He knew all about doubling back. Then, guessing shrewdly, he began to make his way towards Broken Wharf, everywhere asking passers-by if they'd seen a running boy; but it was not until he was in Fleet Street that he met with any success.

'I'm on the look-out for a boy, constable,' he confided to a policeman. 'A boy running away, a boy wanted for robbery and assault.'

The policeman looked interested. Plainly he had seen something. 'Can you describe this boy, sir?'

'That I can, constable. To begin with, he were smallish.' The policeman nodded, and the questioner's hopes rose. 'Yellow weskit,' he went on quickly, 'check trousers, brown jacket, hat with a shiny peak and face very thin and white, like a chicken bone.'

The policeman shook his head. 'No, sir. Can't oblige. The only boy I've seen in a hurry was quite different. He was as black as your hat.'

The questioner frowned. He'd guessed wrong. He went back towards the pawnbroker's to search again. Half an hour later, the *Lady* sailed.

FIFTEEN

Secrets, Barnacle thought bitterly, were just like wind: they were uncomfortable to hold back, and they made a nasty smell if you let them out.

He was crouching on the draughty deck of the *Lady* in a blanket and nothing else. Mister Gosling had done him over under the pump on Broken Wharf, and his empty garments were drying out on a stay-line, like signals being flown for a boy in distress. And if ever there was a boy in distress, it was Barnacle, shivering and holding on to the secret of his blackness with all his might, as the *Lady* sailed downstream.

The business of the pawnbroker's chimney, and the locket, and what he'd been aiming to do with it, and why, was a business he was not prepared to talk about, from motives of both delicacy and fear. You couldn't have got it out of him with a meat-hook, so Mister Gosling might just as well stop trying.

The gent with the apple and the hundred-bladed knife had given him a very bad fright. It had made him wonder if the locket was worth more than even Miranda had supposed. Or were they after him on account of the spoon? Or was it just him, that animal Barnacle, what was wanted, to be made an example of as a terrible warning to boys? Barnacle scowled and hunched his shoulders. Whatever the reason, it was his secret, and, he felt powerfully, it was better kept in than let out.

'For the last time, Barnacle,' began Mister Gosling, leaning over sideways as he guided the *Lady* through the gathering mists and gloom.

'Like I told yer, mister,' said Barnacle, without waiting for the rest of the question, 'I fell down the funnel o' one o' them steamboats, just as it come puffin' out from under the bridge. On me Bible oaf! '

Mister Gosling gave up. The foggy river, the changing wind and the smudgy craft that came and went like ghostly moths were enough to contend with without the aggravation of Barnacle. Mister Gosling was a man who did not like secrets. They worried him. He'd never managed to keep any himself, as he'd never known what to do with them. In his heart of hearts, he'd always felt that there was something shameful and dishonest about secrets, and he was, above all, an honest man. But he was honest according to his own lights, and the policeman inside his head was paid his wages by a different government from the one who paid the policeman on the corner of the street.

'Mister!'

'What is it, Barnacle?'

'Can I put me clothes on?'

'They're still sopping wet. Wait till we get to the Traveller's.'

He stared at the heap of blanket with the little tufted head on top. Although the lad knew his port from his starboard and his sprit-sail from his mizzen, he was still, as Mrs McDipper had said, a child of darkness. He needed schooling almost as much as he needed bread.

'Barnacle!'

'Yus, mister?'

'Do you know your Ten Commandments?' He did not feel equal to beginning with Arithmetic or History or Trigonometry, as he felt it would be a case of the blind leading the blind.

'I heard of 'em, mister,' came the puzzled reply. 'But I can't say as I'm personally acquainted.'

'Then we'll begin with Number One,' said Mister Gosling firmly, when a waterman's voice hailed him, from somewhere off the starboard bow.

'Ahoy there, Tom Gosling! Smell you a mile off!'

'Much obliged, Mister Kemp! What's the weather like downriver?'

'Thick as a plank!'

Mister Kemp passed by, and Mister Gosling returned to Number One.

'I am the Lord thy God.'

'What was that, mister?'

'I am the Lord thy God,' repeated Mister Gosling.

'Can't 'ear yer, mister! Me ears is still full o' soap!'

'I AM THE LORD THY GOD!' bellowed Mister Gosling, this time at the top of his voice.

'That's coming it, Tom Gosling!' came the waterman's voice from somewhere astern. 'That's coming it a bit steep even for a bargee!'

Mister Gosling went red and swore; and Barnacle stayed ignorant as the stinking *Lady* sailed on past Greenwich and towards the Traveller's Rest.

The weather off Gravesend was like Mrs McDipper's cooking: thick, yellowish-grey, and full of mysterious lumps. Foghorns boomed, lanterns blinked and glimmered, and the mysterious lumps turned themselves into looming ships. Alongside one such vessel, and already loaded with wallpaper and china from Hamburg and Berlin, lay the McDippers' barge. The huge ship towered up darkly into the foggy air, and her stern lights gleamed over her name: *December Rose*.

A white face, like a smudge of chalk, appeared over the side and called: 'Are you all secure there down below, Mrs McDipper, ma'am?'

'All secure, Captain O'Shea!' confirmed Mrs McDipper, with a careless wave of her arm and a thoughtless flash of her eyes, for all the world as if she'd never heard of sables and didn't have a daughter to whom she'd given her solemn word.

'Ma!' cried out Miranda indignantly. 'Me sables! You promised!'

'What was that, ma'am?'

'Me daughter,' returned Mrs McDipper, feeling the hopelessness of denial. 'She's set her heart on a bit of Russian sable. I don't suppose you have such a thing aboard?'

But he did: and if the lady would come aboard, she would be very welcome to make a choice. Before Mrs McDipper could make further inquiries, she found herself assisted, with a mixture of affection and firmness, up the ladder that led to the deck of the *December Rose*.

'Ma!' whispered Miranda, giving her another shove. 'Keep your skirt down! You've got a hole in your stocking like a bunch of grapes!'

With a furious look at her daughter, Mrs McDipper billowed up over the side of the *December Rose*. How sharp and pitiless were the eyes of the young, and how eager they were to spy out the frailties of their elders, she thought, and once again wished that Miranda would fall victim to some human weakness and make a fool of herself, so that her mother could get her own back.

Two sailors helped her on to the deck, and Captain O'Shea greeted her warmly. He was about to conduct her to his cabin when he was approached by a tall gentleman in a dark, vaguely military coat and a fur hat. At first sight, he appeared to be wearing a black scarf half over his face, as if he was suffering from toothache, but it turned out to be a beard of extraordinary blackness. He murmured something to the captain, who listened, apparently unwillingly. Then the captain shrugged his shoulders and turned to Mrs McDipper.

'Ma'am,' he said, 'this gentleman, Colonel Brodsky, was wonderin' if you would carry him upriver as far at St Catherine's Stairs. He's worried about the fog delayin' us and he's very anxious to be put ashore.' The gentleman nodded vigorously and smiled at Mrs McDipper. His teeth showed very white and sudden in the black. 'I know it ain't your practice to take passengers, ma'am, but the gentleman will pay you for your trouble' (another nod and smile), 'and, speakin' for meself, I'd be much obliged to you.'

Here, Captain O'Shea spoke no less than the truth. He would indeed be thankful to see the back of Colonel Brodsky. He did not like the man. There was something about him that made the captain feel uneasy . . . something secretive and dark. Already he'd had a visitor, when they'd been anchored off Southend, waiting on the tide; a fellow in a fishing boat, an ugly-looking devil with a broken nose and a scar down the side of his face . . .

Mrs McDipper was doubtful. She didn't like the idea of a stranger in her cabin, but at the same time she felt that the captain was likely to be more reasonable over the sables if she obliged.

'Very well,' she said, feeling irritably that it was all Miranda's fault. 'He can go aboard.'

Almost before the words were out of her mouth, Captain O'Shea had given orders for the gentleman's baggage to be put on the barge; then, taking Mrs McDipper by the arm and drawing her towards his cabin, he murmured: 'And now for that little something, ma'am, that'll put a sparkle in your daughter's eyes!'

Down below, Miranda waited. The night air was chilly, but

no matter! She'd soon have something to keep herself warm! She kept looking up expectantly, dreaming of a cloud of sables and thinking how wise her ma had been to have turned up her nose at Mister Levy's Wapping rat . . .

A bundle appeared over the side of the *December Rose* and began to descend in a cradle of rope. Her sables? No. It was a heavy-looking leather travelling case and a small black bag with a silver clasp. A sailor shouted down: 'Passenger coming aboard, miss! The lady says it's all right!'

A moment later, a dark figure, with a flapping coat, came clambering down the ladder like a huge, ungainly insect of the night. It was a man with a fiercely black beard and a tremendous fur hat. As soon as he reached the deck, he hastened to free his property and signal for the rope to be hauled away. Then, turning to Miranda, he swept off his hat, bowed and announced himself: 'My name is Brodsky, young lady. Colonel Stanislaus Brodsky.'

His hair was as black as his beard, only there wasn't so much of it, and he spoke with a foreign accent as thick as soup. Miranda didn't like the look of him. There was something about his glittering eyes that made her feel uncomfortable.

'Mine's Miranda,' she muttered. 'Miranda McDipper.'

'What a beautiful name!' he exclaimed, with a smile that flashed like bones. 'And so well bestowed!'

Then, before she could stop him, he had taken her hand and conveyed it to his lips for a ceremonial kiss. His whiskers pricked like nettles. She snatched her hand away, and longed to wipe it clean.

'The lady,' said the Colonel, glancing up towards the *December Rose*, 'she is your mother, yes?'

Miranda nodded, and wondered what business it was of his.

'She is a widow?'

'How did you know that?'

The Colonel sighed, and Miranda noticed that his breath smelled strongly of peppermint, as if it had something to hide. 'One can always tell,' he said. 'There is always the sadness behind the smile, and the shadow behind the eyes.'

Miranda looked surprised. The only shadow connected with her mother's eyes that she'd ever noticed came out of a little box and was put on by Mrs McDipper herself.

'She is a very handsome woman,' said the Colonel, and Miranda grudgingly admitted that her ma wasn't bad. 'And you will be like her,' went on the Colonel, with a shrewdly admiring look. 'Perhaps even more beautiful.'

Miranda felt a sudden glow, as red roses came helter-skelter into her cheeks. She'd never been called beautiful since the day she'd been christened in Bermondsey Church, and then it had only been by the parson.

'She's getting me a sable cape,' she said, with a feeling of confusion, and then, as the gentleman glanced down towards his hat, asked, 'Is your hat made of sable, sir?'

'Real Siberian sable, young lady,' he replied, and, putting it on at a tremendous tilt, said, 'It suits me, don't you think?'

He was right. He looked quite dashing in it, and Miranda could almost imagine him galloping furiously into battle and waving a sword over his head. It really was a gorgeous hat.

'So . . . so it ain't Russian sable, then? she murmured doubtfully.

'Siberia is in Russia, my dear. But tell me, how long will it take us to reach St Catherine's Stairs?'

'Depends on the wind and tide, sir. Three or four hours, maybe.'

'So long?' He frowned and took out a gold watch. Idly Miranda glanced at it. Then she stared, and a feeling of weird excitement came over her.

'Show me!' she exclaimed abruptly.

'What? My hat?'

'No . . . no! That watch!'

He looked surprised, and faintly alarmed. Nevertheless he held out the watch in the palm of his hand, but did not unfasten it from its chain. It was open, but Miranda was not interested in the time. Nervously she shut the lid. There was a design on it, a design in black enamel. It was an eagle, and exactly the same as the eagle on Barnacle's locket!

'Well? What is it, young lady?'

'That eagle! I've seen one exactly like it!'

'Where? In the – sky, young lady?' He gave a little laugh, but it had a forced sound to it.

'No! I'm not making it up! It was on a gold locket with some little jewels round it. And there was a picture inside of a mother and child!'

The Colonel put the watch away. His hand was trembling and his air of gallantry vanished. 'Where? Where did you see this locket?'

Suddenly his eyes were as hard and sharp as black nails and his voice was harsh and threatening. Miranda felt alarmed. Her ma must have been mad to let him come aboard and be alone with a child!

'Where did you see it?'

He reached forward and seized her by the wrist. She tried to pull free but his fingers were like iron.

'You're hurting! You're hurting me!'

He let go. He said he was sorry. He begged her pardon and tried to resume his old gallantry. But it was no good. She had seen another side to the fascinating Colonel, and it had frightened her. He was a dangerous man . . .

'Please, please tell me where you have seen the locket?'

'Why do you want to know?'

'It – it is important to me . . . very important!'

She shook her head. He pleaded with her, and his anxious face looked all wrong under the rakish glory of his hat.

'You like it?' he cried, catching the direction of her eyes. 'I give it to you! I give it to you if you tell me where you saw the locket!'

He took off his hat and held it out. She turned away. He accused her of telling lies, of having made the whole thing up, like a foolish child.

'No, I haven't!' she said angrily. 'I've seen it all right. And what's more, I know where it is right now!'

'Where? Where is it?'

She didn't answer. If she said any more, she'd get Barnacle into trouble and there'd be the devil to pay. She pushed aside the hat that he kept urging on her; and then, to her enormous relief, she saw the bulk of Mrs McDipper blooming darkly over the side of the *December Rose*.

'Ma!' she shouted eagerly. 'Me sables! Have you got 'em?'

Down came Mrs McDipper, flushed and trimphant, on to the deck of her barge. 'Here you are, dear, I've kept me word. Real Russian sable for me daughter!'

She held it up. For a moment, Miranda thought she'd got a dead mouse. It wasn't much bigger. Here eyes began to fill with incredulous tears. She'd dreamed of a coat; she'd have been happy with a cape; but the miserable article her mother was holding out wouldn't even have gone round her neck without strangling her! She could hardly bring herself to speak. She was outraged!

'It will make a most charming collar,' said Colonel Brodsky, stepping forward and bowing courteously to Mrs McDipper. 'And if Miss Miranda will permit me to make the offer, it will be very beautiful with this hat.'

Miranda blinked at it through her blazing tears, and heard her mother telling the Colonel not to think of it, as Miranda was only a child and the hat was unsuitable and anyway she'd spoil it like she did with all her things . . . and all the while, there she stood, clutching hold of the stringy bit of misery she'd bought off Captain O'Shea. Miranda took a deep breath. She'd made up her mind and whatever happened would be her ma's fault.

'Ma,' she said, 'Colonel Brodsky's changed his mind. He don't want to go to St Catherine's Stairs after all. He wants to be taken to the Traveller's Rest.'

Mrs McDipper stared. 'The Traveller's Rest? But that's in the middle of nowhere!' She looked hard at the Colonel. 'Are you sure that's where you want to go, Colonel Brodsky?'

Before he answered, he glanced quickly at Miranda. Imperceptibly, she nodded her head.

'Yes, madame,' he said. 'I am quite sure.' Then he gave Miranda the hat.

As she took it, and began to try it on, she felt a little pang of guilt. She'd remembered that when they'd left Broken Wharf, Barnacle hadn't come back. It was possible that he wouldn't be at the Traveller's. Oh, well, she thought, then he wouldn't get into trouble; and anyway, it was all ma's fault. The hat made her head feel like an oven . . .

'Children!' sighed Mrs McDipper, as the barge got under way and the *December Rose* retreated into the fog until it was no more than a dark stain in the air behind them. 'They'll be the death of us yet!'

The Colonel stared at Miranda. His face was sombre. 'I hope not,' he whispered. 'I hope not.' Then he returned to gazing out into the night, while the barge sailed on darkly towards the Traveller's Rest.

SIXTEEN

The parlour of the Traveller's Rest was quiet, as became the ungodly hour; and, not for the first time, Annie the barmaid mourned her move from the noisy, stinking crowded town to the peace of the countryside, which was the peace of the tomb. The landlord who had enticed her away from her previous employment, with an offer of something that might have been marriage, was, as usual, snoring upstairs, while she kept open for the river trade, which was about as lively and interesting as the tide.

There was one snoring loafer in a corner, with his hat pulled down over his eyes; and there was that Mister Gosling, God bless him, for whom she would have stayed open for twenty-four hours, had he not given his heart to that loud-mouthed cow, with hair as red as rust. He was sitting alone and waiting for his boy to get dressed.

Wearily Annie gazed into a mirror that had been supplied by a local brewery and was put up behind the bar. It bore a comforting inscription, 'Beauty in a glass. You and Black Horse Ales', and it wasn't far off the mark. There was plenty of joy left in her: her hair was still gold and her eyes were still blue. So why was she always the Traveller's Rest, and never a traveller's home? Why did they always see the winter in her cheeks, and never the springtime in her eyes? She turned away from the glass.

'Is there anythin' else you'd care for, Mister Goslin', darlin'?' she asked, and then added, hopelessly, 'Anythin' at all?'

Mister Gosling seemed to awake from a dream. He stared at his untouched bread and cheese and pickles as if it was they who had suddenly addressed him and were wondering why he wasn't taking advantage of them. He shook his head.

'No, thank you, Annie. But you might go and see if that lad of mine has got himself dressed yet.'

'Anythin' to oblige *you*, Mister Goslin', dear,' she said, with a contemptuous glance at the snoring loafer. 'Anythin' at all.'

She emerged sinuously from behind the bar and swayed away into the back. She knocked on a door. 'Your Mister Goslin's askin' for you, dear. Are you decent?'

'I got me clothes on, miss,' came the faint reply.

'Hurry along, then, dear,' said Annie, beginning to retreat.

'Can yer come in, miss?' came the voice again, anxiously. 'I want to show yer somefink.'

Annie paused. Then sighed and shook her golden head. 'Well, reely! You naughty boy, you!' she said, more from force of habit than feelings of reproach. 'Just a peep, then.'

She opened the door. Barnacle, in his still-damp clothes, was a sad and crumpled sight, as if someone had screwed him up and tried to throw him away.

' 'Ere, miss!' he said, somewhat shyly. 'Wotcher fink?'

He held out a golden locket on a chain. She stared at it. Her eyes widened in surprise.

'Oh my!' she murmured, half-wondering if the child was going to give it to her. 'That's reely luvly! Where did you get it, dear?'

'Me ma give it to me,' said Barnacle, and showed Annie the picture inside. 'Look! That's me an' 'er when I was little!'

'Oo! You little fibber, you!' cried Annie, really shocked by the blasphemous nature of Barnacle's claim. 'That's a 'oly picture! You nicked it, didn't you?'

'No, I didn't,' said Barnacle, not even trying to sound indignant, as he had got used to nobody ever believing that he could own anything worth money. 'Miss Miranda said you used to work for a pawnbroker and you'd know 'ow much it's worth. 'Ow much, miss?'

'Well . . . I don't know,' said Annie, looking carefully at the locket and trying to remember what her previous employer would have said. 'If it's reel gold . . . and them's reel diamonds . . . well, reely, I wouldn't care to say off-hand . . .'

' 'Leven pound?' suggested Barnacle.

'Well,' began Annie, putting out the tip of her tongue to help her think, when there came the sounds of customers coming into the parlour. 'I'll tell you later, dear,' she said quickly. 'Got to go now. You hurry along, dear. Mister Goslin's been askin'!'

She tidied her hair, expanded her bosom, and went sinuously back into the parlour, where her welcoming smile turned a little glassy when she saw who the customers were. It was that loud-mouthed cow with red hair, and her daughter looking sick as a mouse under a huge fur hat.

'Why, Clara!' Mister Gosling was saying, jumping up from his chair like he'd sat on a nail. 'What a surprise!'

But the real surprise was the gentleman who'd come in at the same time; and even the snoring loafer woke up enough to lift a blotchy face like a boozer's moon, and take a squint.

He was all in black, and most of all his hair and beard, which looked as if they'd come straight out of a bottle of ink. He stood just inside the door, breathing heavily and rolling his eyes round and round the parlour in a way that made spiders run up and down Annie's spine. She'd never seen such a look! You could tell there was going to be trouble all right. That cow, Mrs McDipper, was heaving away like she'd burst her seams, and her daughter was looking sicker than ever.

'Well, miss? What have you been up to?' demanded her mother; but before the girl could say anything, even supposing she was in a state to, the gentleman gave her such a glare that you couldn't help feeling sorry for her, no matter what she'd done.

'Well?' he asked her in a terrible, foreign voice. 'Where is she? Where is the lady?'

'Lady? Lady? What's all this about, miss?' shouted Mrs McDipper, looking as if she was going to fetch her daughter a clout round the ear, while poor Mister Gosling just stood there, with his eyes and mouth wide open and as bewildered as Annie.

'Is the gentleman lookin' for a lady?' asked Annie, feeling that it was her place to spread peace and goodwill and keep up the reputation of the Traveller's Rest. 'Was it any lady, sir . . . or was it one in particular?'

Nobody took any notice, and Annie was just going to restore her strength with a nip of gin, when the girl's face suddenly changed and her eyes shone like sixpences!

'He's got it!' she screeched out in a voice that went right through you. 'Barnacle! The locket! Show him that locket!'

Everybody looked, and there he was, right up against the bar. He'd just come in, poor, crumpled little soul! and was looking as though he wished he hadn't. You felt that if there'd been a crack in the floorboards worth mentioning, he'd have gone right through it.

'Locket? What locket, miss?' he mumbled, his tongue coming out like a little pink flower to wet his lips. 'I – I dunno wotcher mean!'

They were all staring at him and, worst of all, the gentleman with the black beard; and he seemed to get smaller and smaller except for his eyes, which had gone as huge as his waistcoat buttons. Then they all started shouting at him about the locket – all except for poor Mister Gosling, who didn't know where to put himself and was looking half worried to death.

'What locket? I ain't got no locket! I never see'd no locket!' wailed Barnacle, holding up his hands as if he was trying to push the whole world away. 'On me Bible oaf! '

'It's no use, lad,' said Mister Gosling suddenly. 'You'd better show it!'

Barnacle looked at him in horror, and there was such bottomless disappointment in his eyes that it must have broken Mister Gosling's heart, and Annie couldn't bear it for another moment.

'You're a little fibber!' she said to the boy. 'What was it you were showin' me just now? A elephant? Come along with you! It's in your pocket right now. That gold locket with the picture inside.'

Barnacle was trapped. He was in a dead end. But still there was something inside of him that stopped him just giving up the ghost. Though he might not have been any better than an animal, he was certainly no worse. If he had to go down, he would go down fighting.

'Oh!' he said with an air of genuine astonishment. 'Did yer mean *that* locket, then?' And he took it out.

Silently the stranger took it from him, and compared it with his gold watch. The two black eagles were exactly alike; there was not a feather to choose between them. He put away his watch and opened the locket.

'It's –' began Barnacle, and stopped. The stranger was staring at him, and there was a look in his eyes that made Barnacle turn over inside.

'Where did you get this? Where did you steal it?'

'I – I never stole it, mister! I never did –'

'The lady! She had it. You stole it from her!'

'No, mister! No! There weren't no lady! As Gawd's me witness, there weren't no lady!'

'He's telling the truth, sir,' said Mister Gosling, moving beside the boy as if to protect him. 'Can't you see that? He's telling the truth, I say.'

'Then where did he get it?' almost shouted the stranger, staring at the locket as if it was something terrible. 'You must tell me, child! It is a matter of life and death!'

At the word 'death', the parlour was silent, as they say happens when a dark angel passes overhead; and Barnacle felt more frightened by the quiet than by all the shouting before.

'I never took it orf no lady . . . I never did,' he whispered unhappily. 'Nicked it orf a table, didn't I, in a big 'ouse. Fell down the chimney, didn't I, and come out into this room . . . an' there they all was, starin' at me –'

'Who was staring at you, boy?'

'There was Fat-Guts, an' Smooth-an'-Bony, an' there was old Whistlin' Edge, what was the worst. An' they started comin' at me, so I 'ad to frow fings, didn't I? An' when there weren't no more to frow, I nicked what I could orf the table, which were this 'ere locket an' a fistful o' spoons . . . an' then I went froo the winder like a dose o' salts, didn't I? An' that's the troof, mister, strike me dead if it ain't!'

'Who were these people . . . this – Fat-Guts and – and –'

'Dunno, mister. Never stopped to find out. All I knows is that one of 'em, old Whistlin' Edge, were a pleeceman. Inspector Creaker, they called 'im –'

'*Creaker!*' The word came out like someone had stuck a knife in the man, and if there hadn't been a chair to save him, he'd have gone straight down on the floor. Never in all her life had Annie seen a gentleman so shaken; and she was torn between going for some brandy or staying to find out more.

'Oh my God, oh my God!' he kept on saying, and then going off into his own language, and then back again into his queer, thick English. 'He must have killed her . . . look, look! The chain is broken . . . such violence! Yes . . . yes, he has killed her . . . that poor woman, that poor woman!'

It all sounded so strange and horrible, and somehow it seemed to be made worse by being whispered and muttered in the peaceful parlour of the Traveller's Rest.

'Come away, Miranda!' said Mrs McDipper shakily. 'Come away, girl! This ain't anything to do with us!'

As she began to pull and tug Miranda towards the door, the gentleman looked up, and you could see he was almost at his wit's end.

'Madame! Please! I beg of you to take me with you! Please!'

'No, Colonel Brodsky, no! I – I am sorry. We've brought you here. You've got what you wanted. We can't do any more. You must understand that we – we are ordinary river folk. We don't want to know anything about – about killings and the police. Come along, Miranda, come along, I say!' She dragged on her daughter's arm, but the girl seemed unwilling and kept looking back. 'For God's sake, girl!' she urged, 'and – you too, Mister Gosling! Let's get away from this place!'

Mister Gosling hesitated, then, with a deeply troubled glance at the Colonel, murmured: 'Mrs McDipper's quite right, sir. We're ordinary folk and this is no business of ours. Come along, Barnacle, lad.'

Quietly, and very mouse-like, Barnacle followed after Mister Gosling; and, as he passed where the Colonel was sitting, he reached out timidly, and took back the locket that was lying on the table. The Colonel must have seen him do it, but he never tried to stop the boy. He seemed too sunk in his troubles to do anything but sit with his head in his hands.

Everybody had gone outside, and Annie was just going to fetch some brandy, when the door opened and Miranda came back. She ran over to the Colonel, and, taking off her huge fur hat, put it down beside him.

'I'm sorry, sir,' she whispered. 'I'm sorry.'

For a moment, she looked as if she was going to put her hand on his shoulder, but she shook her head and ran outside again, shutting the door behind her.

Suddenly the Colonel seemed to wake up. He stared about him and jumped to his feet. 'My baggage! My baggage!' he cried out in alarm. 'I left it on the deck!' And he rushed wildly out into the night.

Annie stared, bewildered, at the open door. She sighed and, a little sadly, went to shut it. Then she drank up the brandy that she'd fetched for the Colonel. 'Waste not, want not,' she said.

She gazed round the parlour wonderingly, as if she found it hard to believe what had just happened. Everything seemed so very sleepy and dull. Suddenly she realized that the snoring loafer was no longer in his place. She tiptoed towards where he'd been slumped, and peeped under his table to see if he'd collapsed. But there was no sign of him. She scratched her head. It was queer that she'd never seen him go. He must have vanished like a ghost . . .

She looked round again, and her eyes gleamed. They'd all gone off and left that gorgeous hat behind. She picked it up. It felt as soft as dreaming. She looked inside. The silk lining was stained, but not very badly, with black dye that must have come off the Colonel's hair. But it would wash out. She put the hat on and went to the mirror. She could hardly believe what she saw.

'Beauty in a glass!' she whispered, hardly daring to breathe for fear of misting the vision. 'Me!'

SEVENTEEN

The old foreign gent, with his coat flapping and his face as grey as dust, came running down the road towards the quayside, waving his arms and shouting like a madman. He's after the locket! thought Barnacle instantly. He bolted aboard the *Lady* and tried to lose himself inside the enormous haystack on her deck like a frantically darting needle. But it wasn't the locket that the gent wanted; it was his baggage.

'I wasn't meaning to make off with your belongings,' Mrs McDipper said, as he stood, panting and gasping and holding his side. 'I was going to leave 'em on the quayside for you.'

He stared at his heavy leather travelling case and the black bag beside it; then he gazed up at the spreading greyness of the dawn, which made the sky look as if it had aged a hundred years overnight.

'Please, madame, will you not take me with you?' he asked again.

Mrs McDipper shook her head.

'Couldn't we, ma?' put in Miranda, timidly. Mrs McDipper turned on her angrily. 'Haven't you done enough, girl?' she demanded. 'I've said no, and that's an end to it!' She turned to Mister Gosling. 'If you'd be so kind, Mister Gosling, to help shift the gentleman's baggage, I'd be much obliged.'

'You, sir!' Colonel Brodsky cried, before Mister Gosling could so much as move. 'Will you take me? I beg of you!'

'Gosling!' said Mrs McDipper sharply, as if she knew what was going on inside him and wanted to put a stop to it; but she was wrong because Mister Gosling wasn't that soft, and you could tell that he didn't like the Colonel any more than she did.

'I'm sorry,' he said roughly. 'I've got a full load.'

But that didn't stop the Colonel. 'I – I could go anywhere!' he cried eagerly. 'I will lie up there on top of the hay! Please – please!'

Then Miranda started up again and Mrs McDipper looked as if she was going to hit her, but she just shouted at her to stop asking as she was only a child and didn't understand the sort of things the Colonel was mixed up with.

'Please!' pleaded the Colonel, rushing from Mister Gosling to Mrs McDipper and then turning back and holding out his hands as if for pity. 'You must not leave me here! I – I have come so far!'

'For God's sake!' shouted Mrs McDipper, losing her temper with everybody. 'Get them bags off my barge! If we stand about here much longer, we'll lose the tide!'

Colonel Brodsky gave up. He bowed his head and you could see how thin his hair was on top. You couldn't help feeling sorry for him.

'Go on, mister,' muttered Barnacle, sidling up beside Mister Gosling and gazing up at him like the animal he was. 'I'll watch 'im. I'll see 'e don't nick any 'ay.'

Nobody said anything. They were all looking at Mister Gosling. Then Mrs McDipper turned away and stared at the river as if to make sure it was still there. Mister Gosling was scowling like mad.

'It's all right, mister,' murmured Barnacle to the Colonel. ' 'E'll take yer. 'E's like that. 'E took me in once.'

Mister Gosling didn't say yes or no, but there wasn't any

need. There was the same look on his face that Barnacle had seen before, in the Jolly Bargeman.

'You're a fool, Tom Gosling!' muttered Mrs McDipper. 'You're no better than that child!' Angrily, she began to pull Miranda on to their barge. 'God knows what will happen to us all!' she said, turning to stare at the Colonel almost with hatred. 'God knows what we're getting ourselves into!'

Then she and Miranda went aboard, and a few moments later her dark sail billowed out like a thundercloud, and the barge moved away.

Not long after, the *Lady* followed, but a slower rate, under a shortened sail. The Colonel was down in the cabin, and Mister Gosling, frowning and tight-lipped, was astern, behind the hay. The fog had lifted, and you could see for miles under the brightening sky. Curiously, Barnacle stared at the dwindling empty quayside and the empty landscape beyond. Nothing moved, nothing stirred, there was no sign of life; yet, as they'd gone aboard, the back of Barnacle's neck had prickled, as if the *Lady* was being watched by sharp, invisible eyes.

The morning sun came up and stretched out long, black fingers from the steeples, like holy policemen reminding the world it was Sunday and nearly time for God. Then church by spiky church, from St Clement's and St Martin's to Shoreditch and St Mary-le-Bow, bells began to chime until they were oranges-and-lemonsing all over the town.

Inspector Creaker, who had attended early service at Aldgate, walked down Ludgate Hill. His mood was quietly expectant, not so much because of his recent devotions as because of an early-morning visitor to Dock Street, who had brought interesting news. He made his way to a coffee stall near Broken Wharf, where he had a cup of coffee and a few murmured words with a surprising individual; then he walked on, slowly and thoughtfully, towards Piccadilly.

'Catch 'im! Catch 'im! Thief!'

The Inspector stopped. He was startled and still half-absorbed in his thoughts. A pie-seller was shouting and a filthy little urchin was running away, clutching a pie nearly as big as his head.

'Stop 'im! Stop 'im! Thief!'

The urchin was trapped. The pie-seller was behind him and the Inspector was straight ahead. There was no possible escape –

'Are you mad? You let 'im get away!' howled the pie-seller, beside himself with indignation. The man had just stood there like a lamp-post, while the little thief had dodged under his arm and scuttled off like a rat. 'Was you asleep or somethin'?'

The Inspector didn't answer. He was profoundly disturbed. For the second time in his life he'd hesitated and let a thief escape him. And he knew why. It had been because of the terror and hatred in the urchin's eyes, which had been so very like that other terror and hatred that had stared at him from other eyes . . .

He frowned and walked away. He vowed to himself that it would not happen again. There would be no third time. He put his hand in his pocket and grasped his prayer book. As God was his witness, there would be no third time.

He reached St James's Church in Piccadilly and waited, discreetly, a little way down the street. Presently the congregation began to come out, at first in ones and twos, and then in a silken river of laughter and fashion and bobbing top hats.

His lordship was there, and so was her ladyship; and there was that tall, lugubrious Lord Mounteagle with his queer, stooping walk, as if he was afraid of bumping his head against the sky. The Inspector smiled . . .

Lord Mounteagle greeted the great Minister and his lady wife courteously, and exchanged a few words before moving away; and it was plain from the look on her ladyship's face, as she stared after him, that he was a man she thoroughly disliked. Then Mr Hastymite came out, and her ladyship was all brightness and smiles.

'Dear Mr Hastymite!' she cried, advancing and holding out her hand. 'Do you know, when I come out of church on a Sunday, I feel so very good . . . for about half an hour! Ha ha!'

'For a whole half-hour, dear lady?' returned Mr Hastymite, with a wondering shake of his head. 'Then you are indeed fortunate!'

'You wicked, wicked man!' she laughed, and then looked a little put out as Mr Hastymite, having caught sight of the waiting Inspector, begged to be excused.

He signalled to the Inspector to walk on a little, and then joined him when they were sufficiently far away not to be overheard.

'Well?' he murmured. 'You look well satisfied, Inspector. Are we to conclude that you have been successful?'

Quietly the Inspector related the news he had received that morning. The man Brodsky had not gone to the meeting-place at St Catherine's Stairs. It was to be supposed that, somehow, he had been warned –

'Then you've lost him, damn you!' interrupted Mr Hastymite, his blue eyes blazing with anger.

'No, sir,' said the Inspector. 'We know very well where he is. He is hiding on the man Gosling's barge. And if you put yourself in his place, sir –'

'Aren't you asking a little too much, Inspector,' interposed Mr Hastymite coldly, 'for me to put myself in the place of a murderous devil like that, a man whose sworn aim is to destroy everything that has made our country great? Have you forgotten yesterday's outrage already?'

The Inspector had not forgotten. A bomb had been thrown at a Minister's carriage in Whitehall. Mercifully it had missed its aim, and the only damage done had been the blowing to bits of a crossings-sweeper and his dog. But it had been a narrow escape . . .

'I did not mean to give offence, sir,' said the Inspector. 'All I meant was that a man in his situation, having been warned that his plan is known, would not dare to leave his hiding-place until –'

'Very well, Inspector. I am sure you are better acquainted with the workings of the criminal mind than I am. But the funds he was carrying. The money. You know what great store his lordship sets by it.'

'He has it with him, sir. We are certain of that.'

Mr Hastymite nodded. 'You have been vigilant, Inspector. But then we expected no less from you. Tonight, you say?'

'Tonight, sir.'

'And – the boy? You have not forgotten the boy?'

'I've not forgotten him, sir.'

Mr Hastymite sighed. 'I know it's a hard duty, Inspector. But remember the old prayer. How did it go? Something about delivering us all from the traitorous and bloody-intended massacre by gunpowder. That's a prayer to God, Inspector. That's a prayer to the great Judge who sits over all of us. So it's to be tonight.'

'Yes, Mr Hastymite. It's to be tonight.'

EIGHTEEN

Mister Gosling was an angry man. He was angry with himself and with Barnacle. He was angry with Mrs McDipper who had called him a fool, and with her daughter who had started it all. He was angry with Annie, the interfering barmaid at the Traveller's, and he'd lost his temper with the *Lady*, who'd dipped and heaved like a drunken slut and caught his finger against the mooring-post on Broken Wharf. But most of all he was angry with the man he'd taken aboard and who was still down below in the tiny cabin, making himself at home.

He'd not spoken a word to the man since they'd cast off; nor had he said much to anybody else, apart from the gruff necessities of wharf-side business. He was saving his breath to cool his porridge, and his porridge stayed burning hot. When he'd gone down into the cabin to put away the money he'd been paid out for the hay, the Colonel had been asleep in his, Gosling's bed; but now, at last, he was awake and moving about. Mister Gosling breathed deeply, and, telling Barnacle to get a move on with sweeping the hay off the deck, went down below again.

The Colonel was in his shirt-sleeves. He'd found a bit of mirror and had helped himself to a pot of stove-blacking which he was applying, with the tip of his forefinger and by the light of Gosling's candle, to the roots of his beard.

'Ah!' he exclaimed, looking a little uncomfortable and then smiling and waving his black finger in the air, as if to make light of the stolen darkening. 'I was trying to make myself respectable, Mister Gosling! My – my toilet articles are in my travelling-case, you understand! One likes to look young, eh?' He applied the remainder of the blacking on his fingertip to his beard. 'One likes to forget what a bad bargain one has made to have exchanged the gold of youth for the silver of age! A little harmless vanity, eh?'

The frightened, desperate man on the quayside seemed to have vanished, and in his place there was only a vain, elderly gentleman. But Mister Gosling was not entirely taken in.

'Nobody minds a bit of harmless vanity, Colonel Brodsky,' he grunted, feeling that behind the Colonel's easy eyes there lurked a very sharp brain indeed, 'if that's the one harmless thing about you.'

The Colonel turned away, and the only sound was that of Barnacle, with his busy broom, up above.

'You do not like me,' murmured the Colonel, gazing a little sadly into the mirror. 'I know it.'

'I'd sooner put it that I don't like what you're up to, Colonel Brodsky.'

'What? My beard, do you mean? Would you like me better if I was grey, like an old wolf?'

'I didn't meant that, Colonel Brodsky,' said Mister Gosling, disliking the man more and more for treating him like a child. 'Although now you come to mention it, I'd sooner see a man in his true colours . . . and maybe wolf ain't so far from the mark.'

'So what is it that you do not like, Mister Gosling?' asked the Colonel, putting on his jacket and smoothing back his hair.

'I don't like the way you keep down here as if you're frightened to show your face, Colonel Brodsky. I don't like all that talk about killings and the police. To put it plain, I don't trust you, Colonel Brodsky, and the sooner you go, the better.'

Suddenly the frightened man was back again. His hand trembled as he put the lid back on the blacking-pot and returned it to the shelf.

'I understand how you must feel, Mister Gosling. But believe me, sir, there are reasons, good reasons for everything! And I swear to you that I mean you no harm!'

'That's easily said, Colonel Brodsky,' said Mister Gosling, feeling much more at ease with the frightened man than with the other. 'But you're from Russia, ain't you? And there's people who come over here from your country and do a great deal of harm . . . with their bombs in the streets and their blowing to bits of ordinary, harmless folk! But maybe you and me have different ideas on what's meant by harm?'

The Colonel nodded. 'So that is what you think of me,' he said, not in the least taken aback or even surprised by the anger and bitterness of Mister Gosling's words. 'You think I am a violent, dangerous man! You think, maybe, I have come here to – to blow up your Parliament! You think I am an enemy of your people!'

'You know best what you are, Colonel Brodsky.'

'Yes, I know it,' said the Colonel after a pause, during which it was plain that he was thinking carefully of how to choose his words. 'But you do not. And that is very interesting to me, Mister Gosling.'

'Why?'

'Because you have given me shelter. Because, even though you thought I had come to break your laws, to do terrible things, you took me aboard your ship . . .'

'Maybe I did wrong, then,' said Mister Gosling uneasily. 'Maybe if I'd thought about it, I would have left you there . . . but – but –'

'But what, Mister Gosling?'

'But you was alone,' Mister Gosling came out with uncomfortably, and feeling that reasons which had seemed strong at the time now sounded more like the excuses of a child, 'and you was a very frightened man.'

'And that was enough for you to – to give shelter to an enemy of your country?' put in the Colonel eagerly, and with the air of a man who would clutch at anything to save himself.

'I don't know about that,' said Mister Gosling. 'All I can tell you is that there's a law inside of us all that we has to abide by, and sometimes it's a different law from the law of the land.'

The Colonel breathed a sigh of relief. 'I thank you, Mister Gosling; and, believe me, I honour you for your reasons. But – but –'

'But what, Colonel Brodsky?'

'I am still alone, Mister Gosling, and I am still a frightened man. Will you let me stay here until it is dark?'

Mister Gosling hesitated. He bit his lip. The Colonel had got the better of him, and the man knew it. He was smiling . . . Suddenly Mister Gosling became aware that the sounds of sweeping had stopped.

'Barnacle!' he shouted angrily.

Instantly there was the startled gasp of an eavesdropper, followed by the furtive creak of a hurried departure from the hatch. Then, from a respectable distance, and accompanied by a noise of violent sweeping, came Barnacle's voice: 'I'm over 'ere, mister!' There was a patter of running feet, and Barnacle, devotedly clutching his broom, came down the ladder. 'Wotcher want, mister?'

'You were listening, weren't you?' demanded Mister Gosling, and with a look that warned Barnacle that there'd be more trouble if he denied it.

'Yus, mister,' he said humbly. 'It's me nature. Can't 'elp it.

It's bein' up chimneys what done it. When yer stuck up a flue an' 'ears voices, you just got stop an' 'ave a good listen.'

He looked down and fiddled with his broom; then he glanced quickly from Mister Gosling to the black-bearded foreigner. The Colonel was staring straight at Mister Gosling in a queer, searching kind of way that filled Barnacle with uneasiness.

'Don't you let 'im stay, mister!' he said suddenly. 'You 'eard what 'e said about breakin' the law! You'll be for it, mister! For Gawd's sake, tell 'im to shove off!'

'That's enough of that!' said Mister Gosling sternly; and then, more gently, he said: 'It'll be all right, lad. The Colonel's going tonight.'

Barnacle shrugged his shoulders. He'd done all he could. He began to go back up the ladder, when the Colonel called him back.

'That locket –'

'The boy's told you all he knows,' said Mister Gosling sharply. 'Leave him alone.'

'The house! The house where he stole the locket! Please, please let him tell me where it is!'

'Why do you want to know?' asked Mister Gosling, moving in front of Barnacle as if to stop the Colonel getting at him with a knife or something. 'Is it another of your matters of life and death, Colonel Brodsky?'

'Yes – yes!' cried the Colonel. 'Perhaps of – of many lives and many deaths!'

'I don't believe you,' said Mister Gosling, and kept making quick, pushing movements with his hands behind his back, to tell Barnacle to shove off up the ladder.

But the Colonel was one too many for him. He was round the side and gabbling away at Barnacle, and trying to grab hold of him . . .

'You, child! You must tell me! Listen! You want me to go? You are frightened for your Mister Gosling? All right – all right! Tell me where the house is and I will go now! At once! You will never see me again! I swear it! The house – the house –'

He meant it all right. You could see he was tearing his heart out over it. But it weren't no good . . . even though Barnacle would have given back the locket to have told him and got rid of him.

'I dunno where it is, mister,' he muttered unhappily.

'But you must know! You went there –'

'I never went, mister. I was took. I was a climbin' boy, wasn't I? An' climbin' boys goes where they're took. I just follered after my Mister Roberts an' 'is brushes. Gawd knows where the 'ouse was. Tell yer what, though,' said Barnacle, suddenly hopeful, 'my Mister Roberts'll know! You just arst my Mister Roberts where the 'ouse was where 'is Barnacle fell down the chimney an' broke a winder! 'E'll remember!'

'Where does he live?'

'Dunno the name o' the street, mister. Never did. But I could show yer.'

'Good! Good! We will go together!'

'No!' said Mister Gosling suddenly. 'I'm not having that, Colonel Brodsky!'

'It's all right, mister!' urged Barnacle. 'It'll 'elp to get rid of 'im!'

'I said no, Barnacle.'

'But – but it is important!' cried Colonel Brodsky anxiously.

'So is the boy.'

'But he will be all right with me. I promise you!'

But Mister Gosling kept shaking his head and you could see that a steamboat wouldn't have shifted him. It wasn't the Colonel he was worried about, it was the people he thought the Colonel was mixed up with.

'I'll go with the boy myself,' he said.

The Colonel began to thank him, but Mister Gosling didn't

want any of his thanks. He wanted to get rid of him as quick as possible.

'I'll fetch your bags,' he said. 'And then you'll be ready to go.'

The Colonel held up his hand. 'Please! Not yet! Later – later. There – there might be someone watching.'

'What? Watching this barge?' asked Mister Gosling, as if he thought the Colonel had gone off his head. 'Nobody knows you're here. You must have a very guilty conscience, Colonel Brodsky, if you think you're being watched all the time!'

NINETEEN

The out-of-work youth on Broken Wharf slouched and shuffled over the cobbles, whistling, *'Oh, dear, what can the matter be?'* as if he didn't much care. He'd not earned a penny all day, and now evening was coming on and the wharf was as dead as a church, except for them two young 'uns off the barges, hopping about as bright and nosy as a pair of parrots . . .

'Where are you goin', miss?' inquired Barnacle, watching with interest as a green and yellow Miranda, fluttering pink ribbons, twinkled across the McDippers' deck. 'Tea wiv the bleedin' queen?'

'Little boys,' said Miranda coldly, 'should be seen and not heard. And I ain't so sure about the "seen". As it happens, I'm goin' up to the public house to get a lemon for Colonel Brodsky's tea. Ma says that's the way they drink it in Russia.'

'Then you'll 'ave to 'urry, miss!' he called out as she went over the side with a hoist of her skirts and a flash of striped stockings. ''E'll be gone as soon as me an' Mister Goslin' comes back!'

She gave him an angry look, but nevertheless went on up the wharf at a fair gallop. A moment later, Mrs McDipper's head came up out of her cabin like a bonfire.

'Miranda!' she shouted. 'Where's that girl gone?'

'She's gone to the pubic 'ouse, missus,' obliged Barnacle. 'She's gone to get a lemon for old Brodsky's tea, like you told 'er.'

'Me?' exclaimed Mrs McDipper, looking bewildered and clutching at her hair like a wasp had got into it. 'I never told her! Oh, the silly little minx! I do believe she fancies him!'

'What? Fancies that old gent?' cried Barnacle, staggered by the weird choosiness of the female mind. ''E's old enough to 'ave both feet in the grave!'

'Tell her –' began Mrs McDipper, then she shook her head and vanished, with a look that was half angry and half amused.

Barnacle scowled and hoped they wouldn't have no lemons at the public house and that Mrs McDipper would find occasion to clock Colonel Brodsky one with her frying pan. He wished with all his heart that they'd gone to Mister Roberts hours ago, so that the Colonel would have been gone by now. But there wouldn't have been any sense in it, as Mister Roberts never got out of bed till Sunday was nearly over, and then he went off to church for an hour and came back full of booze and hymns.

'Oh dear, what can the matter be?' went on the youth, and Barnacle muttered irritably, 'Don't you know no other chune?'

At last Mister Gosling clumped up on deck and it was time to go.

'I'll wait outside in the street for yer, mister,' said Barnacle. 'If 'e gets so much as a whiff of me 'e'll 'ave me back. 'E's got me papers.'

'Don't you worry, lad,' said Mister Gosling. 'I'll buy your papers if needs be. Anyway, he's broke the law by sending you up a chimney, so I don't think he'll be that anxious about his rights.'

'I believes yer, mister,' said Barnacle. 'But just to be safe, I'll stay on the other side of 'is door.'

Mister Gosling said there wasn't any need and it would be better to have things out in the open and get them over and done with; which made Barnacle shake his head and say that Mister Gosling didn't know the half of Mister Roberts whereas he, Barnacle, knew him like the back of his hand; to which Mister Gosling replied that Barnacle had never even seen the back of his hand till after it had been washed; and so, still arguing, they left the wharf.

Mournfully, the youth watched them go:

'Oh dear, what can the matter be?
Johnny's so long at the fair . . .'

Suddenly his sad face brightened and his whistle grew as chirpy as a sparrow's.

'He promised he'd buy me a bunch of blue ribbons,
He promised he'd buy me a bunch of blue ribbons,
To tie up my bonny brown hair!'

His change of mood had been brought about by the return of Miranda. She came skipping along over the cobbles, clutching a lemon and looking as if Johnny had spent his last penny on her at the fair. Then she slowed down. Her sparkle went out and she climbed on to the barge like wet washing. Her ma was waiting for her, all in black and carrying a prayer book.

'Time for church, my girl,' said Mrs McDipper.

Miranda faltered and came over faint. She put her hand to her forehead. 'I – I ain't going, ma.'

'What do you mean, you're not going, miss?'

'I – I feel sick, ma.'

Mrs McDipper frowned and looked at her daughter very closely. 'You don't look sick to me, my girl,' she said sternly.

'I've got a headache, ma. And anyway, somebody's got to stay and look after Colonel Brodsky's baggage.'

'Are you sure it's Colonel Brodsky's *baggage* you want to look after, Miranda?' asked Mrs McDipper shrewdly.

'Yes, ma! Honest, ma! Besides, what if he wants something when there's nobody here?'

'Then he can wait.'

'But, ma, my headache's really awful!'

Mrs McDipper put her hand to her daughter's brow. Then she took it away, apparently undamaged by any remarkable heat. She looked in her daughter's eyes; then she looked at the lemon. She sighed.

'All right, my girl, I suppose it's got to run its course.'

'What, ma? Me headache?'

'No, child. Your heartache.' She smiled faintly, and Miranda went bright red.

'It's me head, ma! Honest, it's me head!'

Mrs McDipper didn't contradict her. Poor Miranda really had fallen victim to one of those wild, foolish dreams, those absurd fancies, that she herself remembered only too well. She gazed fondly at her daughter's beribboned hair, and then, telling Miranda not to disturb the Colonel unless he called, she went off to church alone.

As she walked away, she thought how strange it was that, only the other day, she'd been longing for Miranda to make herself ridiculous by some unsuitable attachment so that her mother could pay her out for all her thoughtless, heartless words; but now that it had happened, all she could feel was a great tenderness for her child. She looked back. Miranda waved; and then, remembering, clutched her head.

The youth, sauntering across the cobbles, stopped and gazed admiringly at the pretty girl on the barge.

'Oh dear, what can the matter be,
Oh dear, what can the matter be . . .?'

He was ogling her! How disgusting! He was winking at her and grinning and holding out his arm as if he wanted her to go walking with him!

'He promised to buy me a bunch of blue ribbons,' he went on, putting all manner of affectionate little twiddles round the tune. He was a horrible, thin-faced, rat-like youth, a youth she wouldn't have wanted to be caught dead with.

'He promised to buy me a bunch of blue ribbons,' he whistled; then he grinned like a monkey and pushed out his lips with the offer of a kiss!

Miranda could bear it no longer. She stamped her foot, and, with a look of disgust and contempt, she went down into her cabin and slammed the door.

'Oh dear, what can the matter be?' went on the whistling, mockingly, for a little longer; then it stopped . . .

TWENTY

Mister Roberts sat at his table with a wobbly candle casting drunken shadows all round the room. He was, as usual, consulting his papers, as if to reassure himself that he was an actual person and not just a figment of his own imagination. Suddenly there came a knock on the door, and, as usual, he panicked. 'It's Sundy!' he croaked fearfully. 'Go away! Shove orf!'

The door opened and in came, not the Inspector whom he dreaded worse than anyone, but a huge man who frightened him almost as much.

'Do you remember me, Mister Roberts?' he asked, very quiet-like.

Mister Roberts looked hard. Oh yes, he remembered him all right. He was the great brute what had threatened to black his eye.

'You keep orf me!' he mumbled defensively, and wondered if he could get at the poker in time. But it seemed that the large gent hadn't come to assault the master sweep. He'd just come to ask a favour.

'That house,' he said, 'where your boy fell down the chimney. Whose house was it?'

Mister Roberts panicked again. He'd had more than enough

of that disaster. It had brought that terrible Inspector down on him like a wolf.

'W – what 'ouse?' he stammered. 'There's 'undreds of 'ouses, and there's 'undreds of boys fallin' down chimneys!'

'The house where Barnacle broke the window.'

'Barnacle? Never 'eard of 'im! You got the wrong sweep, mister! Fer Gawd's sake, shove orf!'

No sooner were the words out of his mouth than the door opened again and in came, not the Inspector, thank God, but a small, table-high gent in a yellow weskit, what came up close and looked him in the eye and said: 'Dontcher know me, Mister Roberts?'

He looked, he stared, he squinted, and was prepared to take his Bible oath that he'd never laid eyes on the small gent in his life before.

'But it's me, Mister Roberts,' urged the little gent. 'It's Barnacle, ain't it?'

'Barnacle?' repeated Mister Roberts, amazed out of his wits. 'Nar!' Then, overlooking his previous denial of ever having known any boy of that name, explained: 'Poor ol' Barnacle was as black as me 'at! Barnacle? Garn!'

But then the big fellow came in with both hands thumping down on the table like great lumps of beef and swearing that it *was* Barnacle; so the master sweep, not wanting any trouble, took another squint, and, sure enough, there was old Barnacle's eyes, shining like chips of coal right inside the small gent's head, and, now he came to think of it, it was Barnacle's screechy voice coming out of him!

'Gawd! Is it really you, Barnacle?'

'It's me, Mister Roberts. I been washed, ain't I?'

For a moment, Mister Roberts was overcome. He couldn't get over it. Barnacle! He felt quite warm and fond, and a bit weepy over the reunion. Then he panicked again.

'You shouldn't 'ave brung 'im back, mister!' he cried,

turning to Mister Gosling. 'You reely shouldn't! 'E's dead, you see! When I lorst 'im, I 'ad to 'ave another boy, didn't I? Went back to the orfigen, didn't I? Told 'em that me last 'ad snuffed it. 'Ad to, else they wouldn't 'ave let me 'ave another. It's the law. Look! Look!' He fumbled anxiously on the table and held out a document with a shaking hand. ''Ere's 'is paper. Absalom Brown. That's Barnacle. Deceased. That's dead.'

'This yer new one, Mister Roberts?'

The small gent, who Mister Roberts still couldn't believe was really Barnacle, had drifted over to the fireplace and was gazing down at his old mattress and its new inhabitant, who wasn't much more than a little black twig with eyes.

'That's right,' said Mister Roberts, producing another document. ''Ere's 'is paper. 'Lijah Brown. Just like 'Lijah in the Bible what went up in a fiery chariot. Light a fire under my little 'Lijah an' 'e goes up a chimney brisk as a feather!'

'Cor!' said the small gent admiringly, and Mister Roberts saw that it really was Barnacle, and he rejoiced to see him so prosperous. 'Do 'e talk?'

'Nar!' said Mister Roberts. ''E ain't used to the soot yet. But wotcher up to, Barnacle, now you're out o' chimneys?'

'I'm wiv Mister Goslin' 'ere. I'm in barges, now.'

'You don't say! Well, Mister Goslin', you got yourself an interestin' boy. 'Mazin' powers of 'oldin' on. I wish you well with 'im.'

'That's kind of you, Mister Roberts, and, I can promise you, the boy's doing all right. But about that house. Whose house was it, Mister Roberts?'

Mister Roberts stared past his visitors at the door. He could almost swear that the Inspector was outside on the landing, waiting to pounce on him.

'I don't know of no 'ouse, mister, and even if I did, I wouldn't tell you. It's me trade, see? It's none of your business.

You keep out of it . . . and – and keep 'im out of it, too!' he muttered, pointing at Barnacle.

'Please, Mister Roberts, tell 'im!' pleaded Barnacle.

'You shut yer mouth, Barnacle!' answered Mister Roberts savagely. 'You're dead, see!'

'I'll pay you!' offered Mister Gosling.

'Listen, mister!' croaked the master sweep, his voice shaking with alarm. 'I'm a master sweep, ain't I? I got me pride. I'm not tellin', an' that's that! I've 'ad the pleece round, ain't I? They knows the 'ouse and they're the law and you ain't! So go an' ask them if you wants to know. And if you don't want to ask 'em, you're up to no good! Now, I've 'ad my say, so I'll thank you to shove orf!'

Mister Gosling clenched his fists, but Barnacle shook his head.

'It's no good, mister. If 'e's 'ad the pleece round, you won't get nuffink out of 'im, not even if you takes a 'ammer. Like I said, mister, I knows 'im like the back of me 'and.'

Then, on a sudden impulse, Barnacle went back to his old mattress and gazed down on the black little twig with eyes.

'Best o' luck, 'Lijah,' he murmured; and Elijah's eyes grew huge with hope and wonderment that a climbing boy could climb so high.

'I wish 'e was dead,' muttered Barnacle, as they went back to Broken Wharf.

'Who?' asked Mister Gosling. 'Your Mister Roberts?'

'No. Colonel bleedin' Brodsky!'

When they got back to the barges, they were surprised to see both Mrs McDipper and Miranda on the deck of the *Lady*, and plainly having words.

'I told you, miss, not to disturb him!' Mrs McDipper was

saying angrily, and waving her prayer book, when she saw Mister Gosling. 'The girl's been worrying the life out of the Colonel,' she explained.

'I was only going to bring him a cup of tea, ma,' protested Miranda. 'With lemon.'

'She was banging and shouting enough to wake the dead!' said Mrs McDipper indignantly. 'You could hear her right down the other end of the wharf! I felt so ashamed that a daughter of mine could make herself so conspicuous!'

'But his tea was getting cold and he wouldn't wake up,' pleaded Miranda.

'I'll wake 'im, miss,' said Barnacle sourly. 'Too much sleep ain't good for old gents like 'im!'

He went down the ladder and thumped on the door. 'Come on, mister!' he shouted. 'It's time you was orf!'

There was no answer. Barnacle listened. He couldn't hear anything. For a moment, he wondered if the Colonel could have gone already; then he remembered the baggage. He pushed open the door.

'Gawd Almighty!' he whispered, and came back up the ladder without even knowing how he'd done it. He felt horrible and could hardly stand up.

'What is it, lad? What's wrong?'

Before he could answer, Miranda had started screaming: 'He's dead! He's dead! I know it! He's dead!'

Helplessly Barnacle nodded. The Colonel had been lying face down on the floor, and the cabin had looked like a slaughterhouse. There was blood everywhere!

He collapsed on the deck, but nobody noticed. Miranda was screaming and screaming, and Mrs McDipper and Mister Gosling had rushed down into the cabin.

'For God's sake stop that girl screaming!' shouted Mrs McDipper.

'He's dead – he's dead!' shrieked the girl.

'Run and fetch Doctor Norris!' cried Mrs McDipper. 'Hurry, hurry!'

'But he's dead –'

'He will be if you don't hurry! Run, girl, run, before he bleeds to death!'

TWENTY-ONE

The out-of-work youth sat in a corner of a public house near Blackfriars Stairs. He kept staring towards the window. The weather was very queer. There was something wrong with it. It wouldn't get dark. Although the sun had gone and the street lamps were lighted, there was a sensation of inquisitive daylight that wouldn't go away. He wondered if anybody else had noticed.

He took out Colonel Brodsky's watch and looked at it. It was a quarter past nine. He put the watch away and wiped some perspiration from his brow with his sleeve, on which there was already a sizeable damp patch. He was in a state of considerable inward excitement. He glanced round quickly at the other customers to see if any of them was paying him particular attention. So far as he could tell, nobody was interested in him. After all, he was only a poorly dressed youth with a thin, plain face and not worth anybody's time of day. He took out the watch again. It was seventeen minutes past nine. Quickly he put the watch back in his pocket as the waiter was coming with his gin and plate of bread and cheese.

The fellow put down the plate and the glass almost contemptuously; and it was as much as the youth could do to stop himself telling the waiter what a remarkable customer he was serving. He paid the reckoning and the fellow went off. The youth stared after him, as if to call him back. Then he grinned and hugged his secret to himself with a weird delight.

He took a sip of the gin. It tasted as weak as water. He finished it and addressed himself to the bread and cheese. He was enormously hungry. He frowned. The waiter hadn't brought a knife. He thought of calling out; but that would have been foolish, as everybody would have looked at him. Anyway, it didn't matter; he had a knife of his own.

He brought it out from inside his jacket. He gave a little cry and glared at the knife in terror. The blade was still thick with blood! He put it away. He stood up and stumbled out of the public house, leaving his food untouched.

He walked through the streets at a tremendous rate, cursing himself over and over again for his gross carelessness. For a person of trust and importance, he had behaved very badly. Even now he was practically running, just like some frightened street boy who'd broken a window! He slowed down and began to walk properly . . .

In Rosemary Lane there were a pair of ragged, grubby-faced little girls who ought to have been in bed long ago. They were playing a hopping game under a street lamp. He paused for a moment to watch them.

'Land on a crack,' chanted one, jumping like a dirty sparrow, 'Knife in yer back –'

The youth started violently. He couldn't help it. 'What was that? What did you say?'

The children stopped their game. They stared at him as if he was mad, and, with one accord, screeched derisively:

'Mind yer own business, eat yer own fat!
Don't poke yer nose into my best 'at!'

Then they screamed with laughter and scuttled away. The youth looked as if he was going to chase them; but he thought better of it and continued along Rosemary Lane. Presently he came to Dock Street, where he paused, straightened his shoulders, and walked down it smartly until he reached a tenement building, which he entered and climbed up to the top floor. Then, with a rapidly beating heart, he knocked on the door of Inspector Creaker's lodgings.

The Inspector was in his shirt-sleeves and slippers; and, although he greeted the youth kindly, he looked vaguely uncomfortable, as if it troubled him to be found out in the domestic side of his life.

'Sit down, sit down,' he said, indicating a chair; and then, as the youth stared inquisitively at a bucket of thick white paste that stood on the table and a pasting-brush that the Inspector was holding, explained: 'It's the damp, you know, that brings the paper off the wall.'

He pointed up to a corner of the room where the wallpaper, which bore a design of close trellis-work, was peeling away and revealing underneath an old paper with a somewhat wild representation of birds wheeling, diving, and turning somersaults, it seemed.

'Can I 'elp, sir?' offered the youth.

'No . . . no. There are some things one likes to do for oneself.'

The youth nodded and seated himself; and the Inspector, putting down his brush, did likewise.

'Well?' he inquired, leaning forward and resting his hands on his knees. 'What have you to tell me?'

The youth said nothing. Instead, he smiled proudly and produced Colonel Brodsky's watch. The Inspector took it from him.

'Is that all? You took nothing else?'

'I ain't a common thief, sir,' said the youth, with a reproach in his voice that plainly surprised the Inspector, and, so far as it was possible to tell, pleased him, too.

'I meant the bag. I understand it is a black bag with a silver clasp.'

'It weren't there,' said the youth. 'I looked. I swear it weren't there. I did me best, sir. Anyways, that one won't be causin' us no trouble any more. Me sticker went into 'im like into butter. 'E never made a sound.'

'He's not dead,' said the Inspector quietly.

The youth stared. He couldn't believe it. ''E must be!' he cried, and, pulling out his knife, showed it to the Inspector. 'Look! Look! 'E 'ad that much in 'im!'

The Inspector reached for his notebook, which was on the table. He opened it. 'A doctor was called. A Doctor Norris. He stayed for about half an hour in the barge cabin. Then he left. He made no report of any death.'

'But there weren't a breath left in 'im! I swear it, sir!'

'You were mistaken,' said the Inspector. 'It can happen. It is sometimes harder to kill by design than by accident. The man is alive. Or at least, he was. It is possible that he is dead now. I don't know.'

'I'll go back, sir!' cried the youth eagerly.

'Tomorrow. Did anyone see you?'

'Not a soul, sir. Not even the gent 'imself.'

'Good. Now, the bag. It is the most important thing.'

'But it weren't there, sir!'

'Look again. Most likely it was on the other barge, the one he travelled on from the *December Rose*. He must have left it there. But after what has happened, the people will have brought it to him. This time you will find it.'

'Yes, sir,' muttered the youth, biting his lip in shame over his failure. 'I'm sorry, sir. I don't know 'ow it could 'ave 'appened that I didn't finish 'im off!'

'You're young. You're new to the trade.'

'I'll know better next time, sir!' promised the youth, his eyes shining with determination. 'I should 'ave given 'im a couple while I was at it! But I won't make no mistake this time. I'll do for the pair of them, sir, 'im an' that boy! It'll be a good job, sir!'

'I'm sure you'll do your duty,' said the Inspector, getting up and going to open the door.

The youth got up. 'Thank you, sir,' he said as he went to the door, and his voice was trembling. 'Thank you for takin' it so well. You – you've been like a father to me, sir. I – I won't let you down. You'll be proud of me, sir!'

The Inspector waited until he could no longer hear the youth's departing footsteps; then he shut the door and went back to his work. He frowned. Was he imagining it, or had the errant paper descended another inch or two? He sighed, and, picking up the paste-brush, climbed on a chair and once again set about obliterating the intrusive birds.

TWENTY-TWO

Little by little, the quiet watchers, the crouching murderers and the grim, hook-nosed policemen on Broken Wharf turned themselves into wooden posts and empty barrels and drowsy, leaning hoists.

Soon after dawn, Miranda crept up out of the McDippers' cabin and stared towards the *Lady*. Her face was papery and her eyes were like big black noughts. She didn't say anything, but quietly came to join the lonely, humped-up Barnacle on the *Lady*'s deck.

'Been up here long?' she murmured at length, not daring to ask straight out if there'd been a death in the night.

''Alf an hour, miss. It's like a stinkin' stewpot down there.' He glanced towards the hatch. ''E's in Mister Goslin's bunk, Mister Goslin's in mine, an' I'm on the floor. Soakin' wet, too, what wiv all that washin' away of 'is blood.'

She felt sick, but still couldn't bring herself to ask. 'I thought sweeps were supposed to bring good luck,' she said.

'Wotcher mean, miss?' he asked, wondering if she was having a dig at him on account of the failed visit to Mister Roberts; but she meant that it was him and his horrible locket what had brought bad luck to the Colonel.

''E'd never 'ad knowed about me locket if you 'adn't told

'im,' said Barnacle indignantly. 'Anyway, 'e *is* lucky. The doctor said so. Said 'e was lucky to be alive.'

'Then he's all right?' cried Miranda eagerly.

Barnacle shrugged his shoulders. 'Just about 'angin' on, miss,' he said, with a grudging air, not because he really wanted the Colonel to die, but because he was reasonably sure that if it had been him, Barnacle, what had been knifed, Miranda bleeding well wouldn't have been up at dawn to find out if *he* was still alive! 'Leastways,' he added, ''e was the last time I 'ad a look.'

'But that was half an hour ago! You'd better go and look again!'

'But the doctor'll be 'ere soon,' he protested, and pointed out that, if, as she feared, the Colonel had already popped his clogs, there wasn't nothing nobody could do about it any more. But she kept on and on at him, so at last he went down to have a look and came back with the news that, although the Colonel's face was as white and shiny as a plate, he was still hanging on.

Soon after six o'clock, when Broken Wharf had woken up and was busy with Monday morning, Doctor Norris came into view, walking briskly in his chimney-pot hat, and tapping the cobbles importantly with his stick, as if requiring them to cough and say, 'Ninety-nine.'

He was a gruff, grizzled, snappish gentleman who looked upon the healthy as a shiftless lot of idlers, merely putting off the evil hour of when they would need his services. He halted when he came to the *Lady* and looked inquiringly at the two young persons on the deck. He observed no signs of dismay on their faces, so he diagnosed that his patient had survived the night. He stepped aboard.

'Do you think he'll be all right, Doctor Norris?' asked Mrs McDipper's daughter, whom, the doctor dimly recollected, he had brought into the world.

'Do you want my professional opinion, young lady?' he inquired, removing his hat, which was too tall to go into the cabin. She nodded. 'Very well. I will tell you this. If his heart keeps beating, he will live. But if it stops, then I cannot answer for him. There! And I've a good mind to charge you a guinea for a consultation fee!'

He went down into the cabin, where he was anxiously greeted by Gosling and Mrs McDipper, who ought to have had more sense than to drench herself with scent so that one was almost suffocated by the stench of carnations. However, his business was with the sick. He examined his patient, who was now conscious and gazed at him enormously.

'Well, doctor?' asked Gosling.

'By no means "well",' returned Doctor Norris sharply. 'When a man has had a knife thrust into his back, he cannot be expected to be well. In fact, last night when I was summoned, I would not have given fourpence for his life.'

'And – and now?' It was the sick man who spoke. Although there was considerable anxiety in his eyes, and he must have been in considerable pain, he was commendably calm.

'And now,' said Doctor Norris, in an altered tone of voice, 'I think we may venture, say, six and eightpence. You are a very fortunate man, sir. Had you not been so vain as to be wearing a corset, which deflected the blow, your business would not have been with a physician, but with an undertaker.'

'Then . . . there will be no – no disability?'

'No more than with any other man of your age,' said Doctor Norris, then, as his patient looked distressed at so blunt a reminder of his years, he said gruffly: 'Come, come, sir! You have made old bones! Be proud of them!'

The sick man smiled ruefully, and the doctor thought that, considering he was a foreigner, the man was behaving with some dignity and courage. Suddenly a look of alarm came into his eyes. The doctor bent over him, fearing that some new bleeding had taken place.

'Please!' he muttered. 'You have told no one? You have not reported this – this business to the – the police?'

The doctor stood back. He would have been offended had he not remembered that the man was a foreigner, and sick.

'My dear sir,' he said. 'I mind my own business, and my business is the health of my patients. Exactly how you came by your injury is your concern. It is the injury alone that is mine. I would not expect a lawyer to meddle with his client's digestion; and a physician, sir, does not concern himself with his patient's business with the police.'

'Thank you – thank you! You are a good man!'

'I am a good doctor,' said Doctor Norris, who preferred to be praised for his skill and not his nature. 'Whether or not I am a good man is my own business. And God's.'

He put away his instruments in his bag, snapped it shut and addressed himself to Gosling and Mrs McDipper. His patient was to have nothing solid. A little beef broth and some soup. He was not to be moved. Absolute rest and quiet. He was not to trouble himself about his affairs, as agitation of the mind agitated the blood. 'I will call again tomorrow,' said the doctor.

'My bag – my bag!' cried out the patient with such urgency as to endanger his life.

'Absolute rest and quiet!' commanded the doctor. 'Forget about your bag . . . or, I promise you, you will have no further need of it!'

'But I wish to pay –'

'Come, come, sir! I am not such a skinflint as to worry a sick man for my fee! Mr Gosling here will attend to everything. Mr Gosling,' he said, turning to the great lumpish bargee who stood, not knowing where to put himself, 'it will be three guineas, and that will include tomorrow's visit.'

'Three guineas?' gasped Mrs McDipper, as if she had never heard of such a sum when he, Doctor Norris, had seen her in church dressed like a duchess!

'It's all right, it's all right, Clara,' said Gosling, going very red. He took down a tin box from a shelf and counted out the money.

'Thank you, Mr Gosling,' said Doctor Norris, confirming the amount and pocketing it. Then, taking his leave, he couldn't help observing that Mrs McDipper was rather pale. 'I trust you are in good health, ma'am?' he inquired. 'You are looking a little poorly. If I were you, I'd take –'

'Don't tell me! Don't tell me!' she cried. 'I can't afford it! Three guineas indeed!'

The doctor shrugged his shoulders and climbed up on deck. He frowned angrily. As he'd suspected would happen when he'd left them behind, the two young persons had been playing the fool with his hat and stick.

'I'll trouble you to keep your livestock to yourself, young man!' he said, removing his hat from Barnacle's head, where it had gone down as far as his shoulders.

'She done it, mister!' cried the boy defensively. 'It were 'er idea!'

'Listen, young man,' said Doctor Norris, examining his hat carefully before putting it on his own head. 'I'll give you a piece of advice, and I won't charge you a penny for it. The only time a gentleman gives away a lady is when he's her father and he gives her away in marriage. At all other times, a gentleman holds his tongue. Good day to you both.'

He stepped ashore and walked away, tapping the cobbles as he went. He'd not gone above a dozen yards before he became aware of a presence that irritated him. A youth with a thin face and hay-coloured hair was slouching after him, with his hands in his pockets and whistling 'Oh dear, what can the matter be?' The doctor turned. 'Well? What do you want?'

'Nothin', sir. I was just wonderin' if there was somebody sick aboard the barge? It ain't catchin', is it?'

'It's a cat,' snapped Doctor Norris. 'Sick as a dog!' He stared hard at the youth, who was grinning all over his face. 'But I'll tell you something, young man,' he said slowly. 'Speaking as a doctor, I don't like the look of you. You've got a sweaty look about you. If I were you, I'd go to bed and stay there. Otherwise, I don't think you'll make old bones!'

TWENTY-THREE

No sooner had Colonel Brodsky closed his eyes – for Doctor Norris had dosed him with some drops to make him sleep – than Clara McDipper flew at Tom Gosling like one of those angry swans up Richmond way, all savage beaks and furious wings and hissings: 'That was your rent, man, wasn't it? You're cleaned out, ain't you?'

'Be quiet, Clara. You'll wake him –'

'You're the one that needs waking, Tom Gosling! You need waking up to the real world for a change! Why didn't you say that that money was all you had and you need it this morning?'

'For God's sake, keep your voice down! You heard what Doctor Norris said. He's got to have rest –'

'Get his bag! He can rest after he's paid you back!'

'Leave me be, Clara,' he begged, and wished with all his heart that she'd leave him alone to think things out in his own way. There was no sense in her standing there in the doorway with her hair all blazing up and telling him over and over again what he knew much better than she did: that he needed the money a sight more than the Colonel did, and that a poor bargee had no business to be playing Lord Bountiful with his rent, when other folk, better off than he, weren't ashamed to ask for what they was owed.

'You make me so angry!' she cried. 'I just don't understand you, Tom Gosling! It ain't as though you're obliged to the man for anything! After all, it wasn't your fault that he got himself knifed!'

No. It wasn't. She was right there. But all the same, it had happened on his barge, and it was him who had told the Colonel he could stay on board. And that had been after the man had said he was frightened that he was being watched. He hadn't believed him; but now it looked like the Colonel had been right and he'd been wrong. He hadn't even been able to oblige the Colonel when he'd gone to Mister Roberts – not that it could matter much now, but it was one more thing that weighed on him and made him ashamed to ask for his money back. He couldn't do it. It was all very well for Clara, with tears in her eyes, to shout at him and call him a fool. It was different for her. *She*, with her wonderful looks and grand manner, could have begged in the streets and stayed a queen; but when you were a Tom Gosling, it came very hard to ask for anything . . .

'I'd lend you the money,' she said uncomfortably, 'but I know that if I did it would be the end of us, wouldn't it, Tom Gosling?'

He nodded. She knew him, all right.

'So what are you going to do?' she asked, sniffing and searching her person for a handkerchief.

'I'll go and see the owners, Clara,' he said. 'I'll tell them I'll have the money in a few days. They'll understand. After all, I've been their tenant for close on ten years. They're reasonable people, Clara.'

'I hope you're right, Mister Gosling,' said Mrs McDipper. 'But, in my experience, there's a limit to people's reasonableness, and that limit's generally money. Is that me handkerchief over there?'

She pointed to the table. Mister Gosling picked the article

up. 'You left it here last night,' he said. 'I was meaning to wash it out, but I ain't had the chance.'

'Miranda can do it,' she said, taking the handkerchief and looking at it distastefully. It was deeply stained with Colonel Brodsky's blood. Impulsively she wiped her fingers on it. 'Look!' she said, holding them out. 'Now we've both got his blood on our hands!'

Mister Gosling shook his head. 'No, Mrs McDipper, I take your meaning, and it's as generous a thing as I've ever known; but his blood ain't on your hands any more than it's on mine. God knows who those terrible people are he's mixed up with . . . and may God keep us clear of them!'

'Eavesdroppers,' shouted Mrs McDipper, coming up out of the cabin so quick that there was nearly an accident, 'hear no good of themselves!'

Then, with a blazing look, she rushed off to cry her eyes out for Mister Gosling, leaving Barnacle and Miranda to wonder if what they'd overheard could have been, in some mysterious way, unfavourable to themselves.

At half past eight, Mister Gosling, wearing his best clothes and looking like he was expecting to be hanged in them, came up and said he was just off to see a man about a dog; and Mrs McDipper, who knew what he meant and had her own opinion of the owners, said: 'A dog about a man, more like it, Mister Gosling, if you're comparing yourself with Rycraft and Meadowbank.'

Then she took a good look at him and said: 'You'd better take the boy with you. It can't do no harm for them to see that you've got a child to look after.'

Mister Gosling thought for a moment, then he said, 'All right,' and told Barnacle to get his boots on; but it was plain from the look on his face that he didn't think Barnacle would be much use to him and was only agreeing to take him because he didn't want any more words with Mrs McDipper, especially up on the deck.

He didn't talk much on the way. Most likely he was saving himself up for the owners, Mister Rycraft and Mister Meadowbank, who Barnacle couldn't help thinking of as a pair of ugly old idols on either side of a mantelpiece, grinning their heads off. Nor was he given the chance to think any better of them, as Mister Gosling left him sitting on a narrow bench in an outer office while he went in alone to see the partners, and shut the door behind him.

It was only a thin door with a frosted-glass panel, and if you'd kept your head down below the glass, you could have heard everything; but it wasn't no good as there was a cashier sitting at a high desk and keeping a beady eye on Barnacle, as if he was a bad half-crown.

'Mister,' began Barnacle, thinking he might as well do Mister Gosling a bit of good by getting friendly with the moneybags; when, to his surprise, the cashier raised a finger to his lips and rolled his eyes towards the partner's door.

For a moment, Barnacle thought he was going to fall off his stool as he leaned over sideways so far; but he kept steady, as if he was used to it; and by the way his ears had come to stick out like plates, he must have been at it for years.

'We understand your difficulty, Mister Gosling,' came a voice, very faintly from the other side of the door.

'That's old Rycraft!' mouthed the cashier, leaning over an extra inch. There was a moment's silence, then came a new voice, very eager.

'Then – then it'll be all right, sir? You'll wait?'

'That's my Mister Goslin',' whispered Barnacle, and was answered by a violent waving of the cashier's hand, both to keep the boy quiet and to regain his own balance.

'Just a moment, Mister Gosling –'

'That's old Meadowbank! Sharp as ninepence. You see!'

'My partner only said that we understood your difficulty. But it seems to me that you don't understand ours.'

'There! Told you so!'

'Wotcher mean?'

The cashier waved and tilted wildly again, like he'd been caught in a sudden gust.

'Mister Meadowbank is right, Mister Gosling. If we were to do it for you, then we would have to do it for others.'

The cashier nodded and made a loop in the air with his finger.

'Slippery slope to bankruptcy.'

'And in no time,' said Mister Rycraft, 'we would be on the slippery slope to bankruptcy.'

'And ruin! And ruin!'

'And ruin,' said Mister Meadowbank.

'But for God's sake,' cried Mister Gosling, his voice almost breaking with desperation, 'this is the first time I've asked a favour in ten years!'

'More's the pity, Mister Gosling,' said Mister Rycraft.

The cashier wagged his head and looped with his finger again.

'Dictates of the heart!'

'But even if we were to obey the dictates of our heart,' went on Mister Rycraft, 'there is still the matter of your tenancy agreement.'

'A legal document,' said Mister Meadowbank.

'We must all respect the law,' said Mister Rycraft.

'Where would we be without it?'

'Where would we be without it, Mister Gosling?' said Mister Meadowbank.

The cashier, fairly bursting with excitement, waved both arms in the air, like a bandmaster.

'Our hands are tied! Our hands are tied!'

'So you see, Mister Gosling,' said Mister Rycraft regretfully, 'our hands are tied.'

'Then . . . then . . .,' muttered Mister Gosling, so faintly that the cashier almost capsized.

'If you have not settled your account by nine o'clock on Thursday morning, Mister Gosling,' said Mister Meadowbank, 'our agent will come aboard the *Lady of the Lea* and take possession of our property.'

'Good morning, Mister Gosling.'

'No . . . no. I won't shake hands with you,' came Mister Gosling's mumbled reply, '. . . seeing as how they're tied!'

Then he came out of the office like a runaway horse. It was so sudden and quick that the cashier went arse over tip, and there was him and money all over the floor; but Mister Gosling took no more notice than if he'd been a fly.

'Come on, lad!' he muttered, getting hold of Barnacle and dragging him out. 'Let's get away from this place!'

As they walked back across Blackfriars Bridge, Barnacle said, 'Brung yer bad luck, ain't I, mister?' and stared down at his boots, as if it was them what had said it.

Mister Gosling didn't answer. Either he hadn't heard, or else he was thinking that Barnacle's boots had spoke the truth but didn't want to say so.

'It were a black day when I run into yer,' Barnacle tried again, 'weren't it, mister?'

Mister Gosling stared at him, and shook his head; but it was more like a flea was troubling him than he was meaning, no, it wasn't a black day, Barnacle, lad. Most likely he was too busy thinking about Thursday, when the *Lady* was going to be taken away from him, than to be listening to Barnacle. He must have been wondering what would become of him when he lost his barge . . .

Barnacle screwed up his face. He had begun to wonder what would become of *him* when Mister Gosling lost his property, as he couldn't imagine, for the life of him, that Mister Gosling would want to keep him any more. It was a real puzzle. He couldn't go back to his old master. Mister Roberts already had another boy; and anyway, Mister Roberts had said he was deceased, which meant dead. Briefly he thought about being dead, which, he supposed, would be like being stuck up an enormous chimney for ever. Then he wondered why anybody had ever said that sweeps brought good luck . . .

'Ha ha!' said his boots ironically.

'What the devil are you laughing at?' demanded Mister Gosling, savagely.

'It were just somefink in me froat, mister,' mumbled Barnacle, and went on thinking about sweeps and good luck, and the undoubted fact that he himself had never brought good luck to a living soul since the day he'd been born.

This had never worried him before. When you was up a flue, there wasn't no room to worry about anything more than an inch either way, but now, as they drew near Broken Wharf, things was different. He'd have given a world of Barnacles (one didn't seem enough) to be the bringer of good luck – even the smallest piece of it – to Mister Gosling. Or at least not to be the bringer of still more misfortune.

When they got back, the cabin was stinking of soup and scent. Mrs McDipper was spooning nourishment into the Colonel till it was fairly coming out of his ears. And she was using Barnacle's silver spoon.

'It's mine,' he said, when she remarked on its being silver and gave Mister Gosling a look as if she suspected him of having nicked it. 'It's nuffink to do wiv 'im. It was me what nicked it, wasn't it? Nicked it along wiv the locket, didn't I? There was a 'ole fistful, but I 'ad to frow the rest away or I'd 'ave been a goner, wouldn't I? On me Bible oaf.'

Then, having cleared Mister Gosling of the suspicion of theft, he stumped out of the cabin and wondered if there was anything else worth owning up to.

TWENTY-FOUR

There was silence in the cabin. Mister Gosling tried to smile over Barnacle's confession, but it was no good. Mrs McDipper was looking at him with such pity in her eyes that it was plain she'd read the bad news about the owners in his face. He turned away, hoping to hide the misery and anger in his heart. Although he was a man who hated secrets, this was a secret he wanted to keep, because he was ashamed of it.

He had been deeply and bitterly humiliated. Rycraft and Meadowbank had treated him with worse than contempt. He'd worked hard and had been as straight as he could all his life. But it had gone for nothing. He was worth no more than his weekly rent. All his pride and human dignity amounted to no more than a smile behind an office door . . .

Vaguely, and much occupied with his own thoughts, he noticed that Colonel Brodsky had taken the spoon from Mrs McDipper's hand and was examining it as if he was a silver-smith. He was trying to sit up, to see it in a better light; and Mrs McDipper had put down the soup bowl and was busying herself with a pillow. Then he noticed that the Colonel's baggage had been brought over and was taking up a deal of room. There was a small black bag with a silver clasp, and a leather travelling case of good quality. The Colonel was not a poor man.

It was not hard to guess that Mrs McDipper had brought the bags over in the hope of stirring the Colonel into paying back the money. But it was too late. Even if Mister Gosling had the rent in his hand, he'd have felt more like throwing it into the owners' faces than humbly paying them their due . . .

'My case . . . my case . . .,' the Colonel was calling out. His eyes were glittering feverishly and his papery white face expressed the strongest urgency. Eagerly Mrs McDipper asked him what he wanted from his case, and even Mister Gosling could not suppress a sudden flickering of hope. He knew that he needed the money, not for himself, but because he had taken a child on board . . .

But it wasn't money that the Colonel wanted so desperately from his case. It was writing materials. He needed to write a letter. Immediately. It was tremendously important. It was something to do with the silver spoon . . . the spoon that the boy had stolen from the house where he'd stolen the locket. Look – look! He held it out, but his hand trembled so violently that the spoon was little better than a silver blur in the air. Mister Gosling steadied it. There – there! On the handle. Do you see? A crest, a family crest!

He must write a letter to a certain gentleman . . . a good friend . . . He would understand about the crest . . . he would be able to find out whose it was . . . Then they would *know*!

'You'll only make yourself worse, Colonel Brodsky!' cried Mrs McDipper, angry and distressed, but he wouldn't listen. He had to write the letter. It was more important to him even than his life.

So he began to write his letter, while Mrs McDipper, protesting all the time that he was undoing all Doctor Norris's good work, held his little silver ink-bottle for him . . . and tried to read what he was writing, upside-down.

Almost enviously, Mister Gosling looked on as the Colonel wrote and wrote, wincing and scowling with pain and pretending it was only because he was searching for the right words. How devoted, thought Mister Gosling, the Colonel must have been to his mysterious business to care so much and to find the strength to carry on with it. It was impossible not to admire him, and to compare his passionate concern with his own dull despair.

At length the letter was finished. The Colonel folded it and sealed it up in an envelope on which he wrote a name and address.

'Please,' he begged, turning to Mister Gosling, 'give this into his hand. Take the spoon . . . Into his hand.'

'Can't it go by the post?' asked Mrs McDipper, giving Mister Gosling a frightened look as if to say, for God's sake, don't get mixed up in this business!

'No . . . no. It is too important.'

Silently Mister Gosling took the letter. As he did so, he felt that he was being drawn into something strange and terrible; but, once having taken the letter in his hand, he felt he could not turn back. He glanced down at the envelope. He frowned.

'A gentleman like him,' he said, 'would never see a common bargee who'd come knocking at his door.'

'Take my watch. Ask for it to be shown to him. Then he will see you right away.'

But the watch was not in the Colonel's pocket. They searched the cabin, but it was nowhere to be found. The man who had knifed the Colonel must have taken it. So perhaps the attack had nothing to do with the Colonel's business after all, but had been the work of some casual wharf-side thief? It was possible, but nobody really thought it to be the truth. Murder and the Colonel were too close and well acquainted with one another to have met by chance.

'The locket . . .,' murmured the Colonel. 'The boy still has it . . . I know. Take the locket. He will see you . . .'

'I'll go now.'

'No. Later, later. He is a – a man of affairs. He will not be at home until later . . .'

How much later? An hour? Two hours? No. Evening, when darkness would be coming on. Wait till it was getting dark . . . Darkness, darkness, thought Mister Gosling; everything to do with the man was dark and of the night . . .

'I'm coming with you!' muttered Mrs McDipper fiercely.

'No, no. It's better that I go alone.'

'Why do you want to shut me out of everything, Tom Gosling? You've shut me out of your griefs and troubles! Do you have to shut me even out of this? Ain't I to have any part in your life, then?'

Just before eight o'clock, Mister Gosling asked Barnacle for the locket.

''Ere you are, mister,' mumbled the boy, holding up the locket. 'And I 'opes it brings yer good luck.'

He took the locket and told Barnacle to stay in the cabin with the Colonel and to keep the door bolted and to open it to no one.

'What about 'er wiv the fryin' pan?'

'Mrs McDipper's coming with me.'

'What about 'er wiv the 'ook, then?'

'Miranda will be in her cabin. Mrs McDipper's told her to lock herself in.'

Barnacle looked uneasily towards the shadowy wharf. 'D'you think 'e'll be comin' back, then, mister . . . 'im wiv the knife?'

'No, Barnacle, I don't think he will. If I did think it, I'd be taking you with me. There's many a thing I'd sooner lose than you, lad.'

He stepped ashore and waited until Mrs McDipper joined him in her Sunday black, and they began to walk along the wharf together. After a few yards, he stopped and looked back.

Barnacle's fears had worried him. Mrs McDipper looked at him inquiringly. He shook his head and they walked on again.

Suddenly he heard a familiar sound, a whistling, *'Oh dear, what can the matter be?'*, and the out-of-work youth came slouching out of the shadows, with his hands, as usual, deep in his empty pockets.

'Ahoy, there!' called out Mister Gosling.

The youth stopped. His face was pinched and pasty. 'You calling me, mister?'

'That's right. Still looking for work?'

'Anything to earn an honest penny, mister.'

'Then here's a couple of them.'

'What for, mister?'

'Just to keep an eye on them barges. See that nobody goes aboard 'em till we get back.' The youth nodded and Mister Gosling handed over the money. 'There, now, Clara!' he said as they walked away. 'Now I feel easier in me mind!'

The youth, clinking the coins in his pocket, perched himself on a barrel. He grinned. He just couldn't help it. 'Talk about payin' the cat to watch the canary!' he murmured.

> *'Oh dear, what can the matter be,*
> *Johnny's so long at the fair . . .'*

His whistling was exceptionally bright and cheerful, and it went through the air like a knife.

TWENTY-FIVE

The letter was to be delivered to a house in Jermyn Street; and the name of Colonel Brodsky's friend was Lord Mounteagle. A great name, and a tall, narrow house with a fanlight over the door that glared down like an angry yellow eye.

'Please,' begged Mrs McDipper, catching hold of Mister Gosling's sleeve as he raised his hand towards the heavy brass knocker, 'promise me that you won't do anything foolish, Tom Gosling!'

'What do you mean, Clara?'

'Don't get mixed up with these people,' she pleaded, her eyes anxious, and her face, under her great hat, full of shadowy dread. 'I know how you're feeling, Tom. I can see all the bitterness that's in your heart –'

'What's that got to do with the Colonel's business?'

'Everything, everything! It's just when you're feeling angry and unhappy, like you are, that you can be drawn into terrible things –'

'I ain't a child, Clara.'

'No, no, of course you ain't! But we're simple folk, Tom. Our world's the river and the barges. It ain't Jermyn Street. These are clever people, Tom. They know how to twist things ... For God's sake, remember that it's the police they're against ... and the government ... That means you and me and Miranda and your boy . . . You've always been straight, Tom Gosling. You've never done an underhand thing in your life –'

'Much good it's done me!' muttered Mister Gosling bitterly.

'But it won't do you no good to change now! Please, Tom, promise me that you won't let your bad feelings get the worst of you! Don't listen to these people! Don't let them twist your mind and drag you into their horrible darkness! If not for my sake, or your own, think of your boy . . . It's him what'll suffer most!'

She let go of his sleeve. She had done all she could.

'I'm only delivering a letter, Clara. I ain't delivering myself,' he said, and knocked on the door.

A servant, in shirt-sleeves and an apron, as if he'd just come from polishing the silver or whatever else went on in great houses, answered the door. He was a queer-looking man for the servant of a lord. He was a short, thick-set individual with a crooked nose and a crooked scar down the side of his face; and, although he greeted the callers politely, there was something about him that made you feel he wasn't the sort of man you'd care to meet with on a dark night. Nor, for that matter, would daylight have improved him much.

Mister Gosling showed him the letter. He glanced at it and held out his hand, saying that he'd see that his lordship received it. Was there anything else?

'I was asked,' said Mister Gosling, not parting with the letter, 'to give it into his lordship's own hand.'

'Can't be done,' said the servant, still holding out his hand. 'His lordship don't see callers.'

Mister Gosling didn't say anything. He fumbled in his waistcoat, brought out the locket and put it into the outstretched hand. The man began to grin, as if he thought that Minister Gosling was trying to tip him; then he looked down and saw the locket.

Instantly his expression and manner changed. His eyes widened; he stared searchingly at the callers; then he glanced quickly up and down the street.

'Come in! Come inside!' he muttered anxiously and, taking hold of Mister Gosling's arm, almost dragged him inside the house. 'And you, ma'am, please, come inside! If you will wait here, I'll go and tell his lordship!'

He began to shut the front door. Suddenly he hesitated, as if a thought had struck him. He frowned and, poking his head outside, looked up and down the street again. Only then, when he'd satisfied himself that the street was empty, did he shut the door and bolt it.

'It's the wind,' he said, observing the uneasiness on the callers' faces. 'Comes down Jermyn Street something terrible. Got to keep it out of the house, you know.'

When he'd gone, Mrs McDipper stretched out her hand for Mister Gosling's. He took it and felt her fingers tighten as if to hold him back from drowning. Suddenly her grip jerked tighter still; and she caught her breath.

'Look – look!'

She was staring up towards a window at the head of the staircase. Above the window there was a painted design. It was the black eagle of the locket and the watch!

'Birds of a feather,' said the servant, returning and seeing the direction of the callers' looks, 'like to flock together. Lord Mounteagle will see you now.'

He was a long, thin, stooping gentleman, grey-haired and with a woollen muffler hanging round his neck, as if he was expecting a toothache and wanted to be ready for it; and his servant, whose name was Joe, never let him alone for a moment. He kept hopping and bustling around him, finding him his spectacles, arranging his chair and even peering over his shoulder as he read Colonel Brodsky's letter, while Mister Gosling and Mrs McDipper, seated side by side on a couch, stared fixedly into the fire, which, although the night was warm, burned brightly in the grate.

'His lordship's a chilly mortal,' murmured Joe, darting to put on more coal. 'It's being so tall. Snow on top all the year round.' Then he went back to looking over his master's shoulder.

'Dear God . . . Dear God . . .,' muttered Lord Mounteagle, deeply troubled by what he was reading. He leaned back and took off his spectacles for a moment. Instantly Joe got hold of them, breathed on them, wiped them and handed them back. His lordship put them on again, and returned to the letter.

'This is a bad business, Joe, a bad business . . .'

He shivered. Joe glanced anxiously at the fire. It was red and roaring. His master was feeling the chill not in his flesh but in his spirit.

'There's still hope, m'lord,' he murmured, pointing to a part of the letter. 'D'you see there?'

'Yes . . . yes. You are quite right, Joe. We mustn't despair.' He took off his spectacles again and this time Joe put them away in their case. Mister Gosling wondered if Lord Mounteagle could have put one foot in front of another without Joe being there to smooth the way for him.

They were a queer pair, this master and servant: his lordship, large and almost motionless, like the black eagle over the window on the stairs; and Joe, short and sturdy, like the wren in the fable, hopping and darting but never straying far from his great supporter.

'We are much obliged to you,' said his lordship, to his two silent, uneasy visitors, 'the Colonel and Joe, here, and myself. We are deeply obliged . . .'

'The spoon, m'lord, the spoon!' whispered Joe, urgently.

'Yes, yes. But, first of all, we must think of our friend. The Colonel writes of a wound,' he said, addressing Mister Gosling and leaning forward with a look of deep concern. 'He tells me it is a mere scratch, but I know him too well to believe that. Is it – is it very bad?'

'It nearly killed him, your lordship,' returned Mister Gosling quietly. 'But he's on the mend, I think.'

'We've had the doctor twice,' put in Mrs McDipper. 'And he's coming again tomorrow . . .'

'Thank God, thank God,' whispered Lord Mounteagle. 'I would never have forgiven myself if it had cost him his life!'

'The spoon, m'lord, the spoon!' urged Joe impatiently.

'Mr – er –'

'Gosling,' put in Joe quickly. 'Mr Gosling and Mrs McDipper, m'lord.'

'Thank you, Joe. Mr Gosling, the Colonel writes that you have a silver spoon that was taken from the same house as the locket –'

Mister Gosling nodded. He took the spoon out of his pocket. Joe darted across to take it from him, but Mister Gosling stood up and walked to his lordship and put the spoon into his hand. He knew he was being foolish and almost rude in ignoring Joe. Mrs McDipper was staring at him as if he'd gone off his head. But he couldn't help it. He wanted to know where he stood in the world. He wanted to find out what was going on, and he felt that unless he got past the sturdy, thick-set Joe, he would be left, contemptuously, in the dark.

Lord Mounteagle took the spoon. He examined it in the light. Joe bustled about and brought him his spectacles again. He put them on and examined the crest on the spoon carefully. He frowned and shook his head.

'Here, Joe,' he said, handing the spoon to the eager little man. 'You are always about the town and take note of such things. Whose crest is this?'

Joe looked at it. Momentarily he widened his eyes; then he handed it back.

'Hobart, m'lord,' he said. 'It's Lord Hobart's crest.'

Lord Mounteagle stared at him. 'Hobart? Are you sure, Joe?'

'Sure as I'm standing here, m'lord.'

'Hobart! Good God! A man like that! A man in his position! What do they call him? The spirit of Old England? I can't believe it! It's monstrous, monstrous!'

'I ain't so surprised as you are, m'lord,' said Joe harshly. 'From what I've heard about the town, Lord Hobart's a man who spends money like there was no end to it. There's his new house in Hertfordshire that's costing a fortune. And then there's his friend, Mr Hastymite. He ain't doing badly, neither –'

'What? Hastymite too? Well, that's not so hard to believe. But Hobart! Well, Joe, now we know . . . now we know.'

'But *we* don't know, your lordship,' said Mister Gosling suddenly. 'We don't know anything.'

'Gosling!' cried out Mrs McDipper, before she could stop herself. 'It ain't nothing to do with us! Remember your promise, Tom, your promise! Your lordship! Don't take no notice of him! He don't know what he's saying! We're ordinary river folk, your lordship! We don't want to know anything about your business!'

She stopped and clutched at her breast. She stared round the room half fearful, half ashamed, from Lord Mounteagle, to Joe, to Mister Gosling . . .

'The lady's right, m'lord,' said Joe, looking vainly for something to busy himself with. 'Ladies generally are. It's best for her and her friend not to know. And it looks like the Colonel thought so too. As the lady says, they're ordinary river folk. They're good people, m'lord, I know their sort well . . . and I like to think they're a sight nearer to being the spirit of Old England than Lord Hobart is. If you was to tell them what's been going on, m'lord, they wouldn't believe you. As I recall, you found it hard enough yourself.'

Lord Mounteagle nodded. 'Perhaps –' he began.

But Mister Gosling interrupted: 'I'd still sooner be told so I can judge for myself, your lordship. I'd like to know where I stand. I'd like to know what it is I've been doing. If it's wrong, then I won't have no more to do with it, but if it's right, then I'd like to do what I can to help.'

'Gosling – Gosling!' whispered Mrs McDipper. 'You fool!'

Joe looked as if he thought so too. He shrugged his shoulders and attacked the fire with poker and tongs till it blazed up fiercely and the ugly scar down the side of his face twitched and twisted like an angry snake.

'Very well, Mr Gosling,' said Lord Mounteagle at length. 'I will tell you about it, because I see that it will be a greater burden for you not to know than to know.'

'Thank you, your lordship,' muttered Mister Gosling, sitting down again next to Mrs McDipper, who was biting her lip and twisting up her fingers as if she was inventing new knots.

'I will tell you about the locket that has brought you into this business,' said his lordship, reaching out for the locket that was lying on his desk and having it put into his hand by Joe. 'And about Colonel Brodsky . . . and about a woman – a poor woman! – who, I fear, has been murdered. I will tell you about a great wickedness, Mr Gosling, perhaps the greatest wickedness of all: of unjust men being thought just, and of men to whom we look for our safety and protection being no better than murderers and thieves –'

'You – you can't mean the police?' whispered Mister Gosling, his thoughts flying to the Colonel's dread of the man he'd called Inspector Creaker.

'I mean the secret police, Mr Gosling. Perhaps you didn't know that we have such a thing in this land of the free? Unfortunately we have. They were formed some years ago and their purpose has been to protect us against those violent men, revolutionaries and men of terror who come here from abroad and commit murderous outrages in our streets. But as so often happens, Mr Gosling, the cure has proved as bad, if not worse, than the disease. Because everything has been secret, authority – secret authority – has passed into the hands of men even more wicked than our enemies.'

He paused while Joe replaced the locket on the desk, poked the fire again and arranged a cushion behind his master's back.

'It first came to my notice some months ago,' said Lord Mounteagle when Joe had finished with him. 'A woman came to see me, a foreign lady . . . Her name was Madame Vassilova. She almost forced her way in here. Joe couldn't stop her –' Joe nodded, and Lord Mounteagle went on to tell how the woman had come to beg for his help. She had heard of him as being a lawyer.

'She came because she knew the sort of lawyer he was,' murmured Joe, gazing at his master with admiration and affection. 'The best and the greatest in the land.'

Lord Mounteagle smiled faintly, then his face grew sombre as he went on to tell of how the woman had sat before him, her face white and her great dark eyes fixed upon him pleadingly. As he talked, his gaze turned towards an empty chair, and his listeners fancied that he could still see the woman, sitting there and staring at him.

Her story was a grim one but not, alas, unusual. Her husband had been robbed and murdered. He had been found in an alley with his throat cut and his money gone. But there was something more. He had become involved, without knowing it, with a group of revolutionaries. He was a jeweller and they had disposed of some jewellery to him and he was bringing them the money. He had been killed and robbed, the woman was sure, by the secret police. She knew a great deal about that organization. She had made it her business to find out. In particular, she knew the name of the officer who commanded them: a certain Inspector Creaker . . .

'A dangerous man,' muttered Joe. 'Like a mad dog.'

'I told her,' said Lord Mounteagle, his eyes going continually to the empty chair, 'that if it was a matter of the police, there was nothing that could be done, that the police were a lawful authority and greatly respected. I told her that, Mr Gosling, because I believed she was mistaken. But she was so passionate in her desire for revenge – justice, she called it – upon this Inspector Creaker that I feared she would make an attempt on his life unless I agreed to look into the matter.

'So I looked into the matter, Mr Gosling, and so did Joe here, and we made unpleasant discoveries. There had been other killings and other seizures of funds, but no single penny of the money taken had ever found its way into the Treasury, where it belonged. In short, Mr Gosling, we discovered that men were being killed and robbed in the name of the State, and the profit was going into private pockets.'

His lordship fell silent. He gazed at the two simple river folk who were sitting on the couch, side by side and wooden-faced, as if he was trying to judge the effect of his words and wondering, perhaps, if Joe had been right and they were unable to believe in such wickedness.

'If what you say is true, your lordship,' muttered Mister Gosling, 'this Inspector must be a kind of monster.'

Lord Mounteagle shook his head. Joe had inspected the Inspector. He'd found out a great deal about him. Joe was very good at such things. (Here Joe found it necessary to sweep up the ash in the hearth.) The Inspector lived modestly and not beyond his means. The money was not going into *his* pockets. It was going into the pockets of his superiors, men who were able to hide themselves under the cloak of State secrecy. *They* were the real monsters.

So a trap had been laid to catch them. A letter was sent from abroad to be collected from the Post Office at Charing Cross. It was a letter that was certain to be intercepted by the secret police. It told of a messenger who would be sailing from Hamburg on the *December Rose*. He would be carrying funds. He was to be met by a woman whom he would recognize by the locket she would be wearing, a gold locket with an enamelled black eagle on the back and a Virgin and Child within. ('Me an' me ma,' thought Mister Gosling with a pang of distress, 'when I was little.')

The woman, in her turn, would recognize the messenger by the same design of a black eagle on the case of his watch. The woman was Madame Vassilova, and the messenger was an old and trusted friend of Lord Mounteagle, a brave man who hated injustice as much as his lordship did: Colonel Brodsky.

Madame Vassilova understood the danger she would be in; she knew that the Inspector would stop at nothing to obtain possession of the funds; but such was her love for her dead husband that she was willing to risk everything to bring his murderer to justice.

Once the Inspector got hold of the funds, he was to have been followed; and when he handed over the money to his superiors, he would have destroyed both himself and them.

But he had acted more swiftly than had been anticipated. He must have killed the woman soon after she had received the letter; and, had it not been for the boy – the boy –

'Barnacle!' whispered Mister Gosling, and saw again, in his mind's eye, the scrubbed and frightened child, clutching the locket and the spoon in his fist and telling his wild and childish lies . . .

'So now you know, Mr Gosling,' Lord Mounteagle was saying, but Mister Gosling was still thinking of Barnacle – Barnacle helplessly caught up in these terrible happenings, Barnacle, whose innocent thieving had reached out so far that it had touched the lives of great and important men . . . Then he thought, with a sudden chill, if what he'd heard had been true, then Barnacle was in danger of his life . . .

Abruptly he stood up. He had to get back, quickly! He was frightened. 'The locket, m'lord . . . Can I take it? The boy . . . Barnacle . . . he sets great store by it.'

Once outside in the street, Mister Gosling began to walk with tremendous strides, and Mrs McDipper found it hard to keep up with him. She clutched at his arm.

'So . . . so you believe them, Tom?' she asked, looking at him almost sadly, as if she sensed that he was drifting away, out of her reach, towards some rushing disaster. 'I warned you . . . I warned you that they were clever people who could twist anything . . .'

He shook his head but did not slacken his pace. 'Thank God,' he muttered, 'thank God I gave that lad a couple of coppers to watch the barges!'

TWENTY-SIX

'Oh dear, what can the matter be . . .?'

'Don't 'e know no other chune?' thought Barnacle, as the endless whistling drifted over the wharf and down into the cabin. It irritated him – not only because of the tune, but because he didn't want nobody to be about.

He'd got his eye on the Colonel's black bag. He'd already looked in the other one, and there'd been nothing but clothes and brushes and suchlike. But the black bag had clinked when he shifted it; and the clink, Barnacle would have taken his Bible oath on it, had been the clink of money.

The Colonel was dozing, and it was in Barnacle's mind, just as soon as the whistler had shoved off, to take the bag up on deck and help himself to the needful. Then – and he'd thought it all out while he'd been picking his nose in a corner – he was going to take it to Rycraft and Meadowbank and pay off their wobbly cashier. He hadn't thought any further than that; but then he'd never seen the sense in thinking of much more than an hour ahead. After all, you might fall down a hole in the road . . .

'Oh dear, what can the matter be . . .?'

'Now look what 'e's bleedin' well done!' cursed Barnacle silently, as the Colonel opened his eyes.

''Ow are yer, mister?'

'A little stronger . . . a little stronger,' murmured the Colonel. 'Are they back yet?'

'Not yet, mister.'

'Johnny's so long at the fair . . .'

The Colonel frowned. 'I have heard that before.'

'I ain't surprised, mister. 'E never stops.'

The Colonel shook his head and his frown deepened, as if the whistling was associated with something unpleasant that he couldn't quite remember. 'The young lady . . . Miss Miranda,' he said, 'where is she? Has she gone with her mother?'

'No, mister. She's in 'er cabin.'

'Ah! A beautiful girl!' sighed the Colonel. 'She will break many hearts!'

'If she catches 'em wiv 'er 'ook, she will!' said Barnacle sourly. 'She's soft on you, mister.'

'I know it, I know it,' confessed the Colonel, sadly stroking his beard. 'It is always the way . . . the fascination of the – the older man.'

''Ow old are yer, mister?' asked Barnacle, staring hard at the Colonel's black beard, which had gone a bit streaky from Mrs McDipper's soup.

'Older than I look,' admitted the Colonel. 'A beard, you know, covers a multitude of sins. But when I was younger,' he went on, his eyes shining like lamps in a fog, 'ah! I could tell you some stories, wonderful stories of forests, and wolves, and duels, and battles! Do you like stories, Barnacle?'

The Colonel's eyes were getting foggier. He was drifting off . . .

'He promised to buy me a bunch of blue ribbons . . .'

The Colonel jerked awake. 'Do you like stories, Barnacle?'

'Dunno, mister. Never 'eard any.'

'How sad that is! Stories, my child, are like candles in the mind. They comfort us and show us wonders . . . wonders. When I am stronger . . . I will tell you stories, Barnacle . . .

such stories. But now I must sleep . . . sleep . . .' He closed his eyes.

'He promised he'd bring me a basket of posies . . .'

The Colonel's eyes stayed shut. He was breathing soft and regular. Barnacle passed a hand over his face, two or three times. He'd dozed off all right . . .

'. . . a garland of lilies, a garland of roses . . .'

Barnacle picked up the bag, and waited.

'Oh dear, what –'

The whistling stopped. Barnacle listened. Not a bleeding sound. At last the whistler had shoved off.

Cautiously Barnacle unbolted the door. He looked back. The Colonel was frowning in his sleep. Most likely the wolves was after him. Barnacle crept up the ladder. As soon as he could see over the deck, he paused and stared hard towards the shadowy wharf. Nobody about. He climbed up and on to the deck, trying with all his might to stop the bag from clinking.

He didn't make a sound. Nor did he hear one. He never saw no shadow move, nor did he see the sudden glint of a knife . . .

'What was that, Clara? Somebody screamed!'

Mister Gosling, horribly white, flew down the steps to Broken Wharf and rushed towards the barges.

'What's happened? What's happened?'

Barnacle and Miranda, thank God, were both on the deck of the *Lady*. They were staring over the side into the river.

'I told you to stay in the cabin!' suddenly shouted Mister Gosling, his fear turning to anger.

'And you too, miss!' cried Mrs McDipper, stumbling over the cobbles. 'I'll put you across my – Oh my God! What's wrong, girl? You look as if you've seen a ghost!'

'Oh, ma, ma!' sobbed Miranda, her eyes all wild with terror. 'He's gone over the side . . . into the river, ma!'

'Who?'

'She saved me life . . . She saved me life,' wept Barnacle, shaking and crying with fright. 'She saved me life, mister . . .'

'He was coming with a knife!' wailed Miranda. 'I saw him! All I could do was to smash him with the hook! He's gone over the side!'

'She saved me life . . . She saved me life . . .'

'Barnacle! Miranda! For God's sake, what happened?'

Little by little, Mister Gosling and Mrs McDipper got it out of them. Miranda had come up on deck for a breath of air, when she'd seen Barnacle come up out of the hatch. She'd just been going to call him, when she'd seen a figure coming up behind him. She'd seen the knife in his hand . . .

'It was all I could do, ma! I had to smash him with the hook!'

'I never 'eard a thing, mister! I never 'eard nuffink till she smashed 'im! She saved me life, mister . . .'

'The lad I paid to watch you! Where was he?'

'What lad, mister?'

'The lad that's always whistling.'

Barnacle and Miranda stared. Their eyes were enormous with disbelief.

'It – it was him. He was the one!'

'I only 'opes you didn't pay 'im much, mister,' sniffed Barnacle, beginning to recover. ''E weren't worth it, y'know.'

Mister Gosling didn't answer. He was staring down into the black waters of the river. Suddenly he felt Mrs McDipper's hand on his arm.

'Don't blame yourself, Tom,' she whispered. 'How was you to know what he was? It wasn't written in his eyes. They were just like yours and mine.'

'But I paid him, Clara, I *paid* him! What kind of a world have they made for us, Clara – for you and me and Barnacle and Miranda? And why, Clara, why?'

TWENTY-SEVEN

The out-of-work youth was out of work for ever. He was past all employing. His dead body had been taken out of the water soon after four o'clock in the morning at Wapping Old Stairs, after having floated downriver on the tide until it had fouled a waterman's oar. It had been carried on a hand-cart to the mortuary in Bird Street, where, after the surgeon's examination, it had been laid out as decently as possible on a bare, scrubbed table in a bare, gaslit room; and Inspector Creaker had been informed.

'We knew he was one of your boys, Mr Inspector, sir,' confided one of the two constables who had attended to the matter, and who now hoped for some words of commendation for their promptness and consideration.

'Yes,' murmured the Inspector, staring down at the youth's silent face. 'He was . . . one of my . . . boys.'

Coldly and remotely he remembered the youth's words: *You've been like a father to me, sir*. Well, well, it wasn't the first time that a father had sacrified a son. Even in the Bible, there was Abraham and Isaac . . . A goodly precedent.

'Nasty bruise, that,' remarked the second constable, putting himself forward and indicating a contusion on the side of the youth's head that had spread out like a red rose. 'Hit on the head and drowned, the surgeon said. In the course o' duty, d'you think, sir?'

'Yes. In the course of duty,' said the Inspector, apparently unmoved.

What was it the youth had said to him? *You'll be proud of me.* They had been his last words, as far as the Inspector could recollect. Well, the Inspector was proud of him. He had laid down his life for his country, as Lord Hobart and Mr Hastymite would have put it . . .

The constable drew back the sheet that had been covering the youth a little further. There was a knife still clutched in the dead hand. Gently the Inspector loosened the youth's fingers and took the knife.

'Regulation issue, sir?' inquired the constable.

'Yes. Regulation issue.'

'Will that be all, sir?' asked the constable, beginning to cover up the youth again.

'Yes . . . No! Just a moment.'

He reached out and held back the sheet. He stared hard at the face, as if he needed to imprint it on his memory. The youth's lips were weirdly pursed, almost as if he was still whistling. The Inspector let go of the sheet.

'That will be all,' he said, and left the mortuary.

'Oh dear, what can the matter be . . .?'

The two constables looked at one another.

'He's a cool 'un,' said one. 'Not a word of thanks, and then he goes off whistling! Listen!'

'Johnny's so long at the fair.'

The Inspector went back to his lodging in gunpowdery Dock Street. He was a careful man. He knew how easily anger and thoughts of revenge could cloud the judgement and corrupt the sense of duty. Yet he found it very hard to suppress these feelings.

He put down the youth's knife on the table and, after a

moment's troubled hesitation, began to mix flour and water in a bowl to make paste. He had noticed that the wallpaper was coming away from the wall again, and in another place. He stood on a chair and began to paste it back, but he found it as hard to control the unwinding paper as it was to control his unwinding thoughts.

He must not fail. In no circumstances must the youth be allowed to have died in vain. Even if he, Inspector Creaker, was in the wrong (and that was unthinkable!), the death of the youth made everything right. He had sanctified it with his blood.

But he, Creaker, was not in the wrong. He was defending his country against evil men. He was securing it from men of terror and violence, from men who, his great superiors had told him, wanted nothing less than the destruction of the State, and from men who (and here his anger rose uncontrollably) had deceived ordinary, simple folk, like the poor bargee and the wretched little sweep's boy, into giving them shelter from the law.

He pasted away vigorously and at last managed to get the paper to stay in place. He climbed down from the chair, breathing heavily and feeling, obscurely, that his success was a good omen . . .

'So you think he is being deceived, this dangerous policeman?' murmured Colonel Brodsky, who had improved enough to be sitting up and eating grapes. ('These Russians must be as strong as horses,' Doctor Norris had said.)

For answer, Joe related all that had been found out about the Inspector: his modest lodgings, his frugal habits, his high reputation and his absolute devotion to duty.

Colonel Brodsky nodded, ate another grape and looked for somewhere to put the pips. Joe hastened to provide one of Mister Gosling's cracked saucers.

Lord Mounteagle's servant, in gaiters, striped waistcoat and coachman's hat, had presented himself on board the *Lady of the Lea* at seven o'clock in the morning with a basket of fruit and two bottles of wine, which he had set out in the cramped little cabin as best he could. Even away from his master he was ceaselessly busy. He had once been a thief and a pick-pocket, and Lord Mounteagle had taken him into his employment when he'd come out of prison, saying that, as the Devil finds work for idle hands to do, he hoped that Joe wouldn't give the Devil another chance. Consequently Joe made sure that his hands were never idle.

'He really frightens me,' said Joe, fidgeting with the Colonel's pillow. 'To my mind, he's a sight more dangerous than the others because he don't know what he's doing.'

He had been greatly shocked when he'd heard of the night's happenings, and was fearful that there might be more in store. When he'd come aboard, he'd felt that the barge was being watched. He'd noticed a gent peeling an apple who seemed to be taking an interest in Joe and his basket over and above the demands of an interest in greengrocery.

'Watch yourself, Mr Gosling,' he said, 'and that lad of yours too.' Then he hastened to reassure Mrs McDipper, who had cried out in sudden fear for Miranda, that she and hers were in no real danger, as the Inspector's attention lay elsewhere.

'This is what he's after,' said Joe, picking up the black bag with the silver clasp and shaking it. 'It's the funds, ma'am, the funds! This is what's wanted – to pay for Lord Hobart's new house in Hertfordshire, I shouldn't wonder, and Mr Hastymite's little presents for the ladies. This is what Inspector Creaker's killed for . . . and will kill again, if he gets the chance! If only he knew . . .'

Then he turned back to Colonel Brodsky, and wished that Mrs McDipper and Mister Gosling were not there, as he felt a certain delicacy about airing such very dirty linen in front of such good and honest people. He confided, in a low voice, Lord Mounteagle's fears that it would be difficult to proceed further in the matter. The Inspector's superiors had turned out to be more highly placed and important than had been supposed. They were great politicians and, as such, would always be able to hide their crimes under the cloak of National Security. Even with proof against them, they could always run into the bolt holes of official secrets . . .

As Mrs McDipper sat listening to the low voices murmuring about these horrible matters, she stared at the black bag that meant so much, and she wished with all her heart that it could be abandoned, even to the wicked men who had murdered for it, so that it would be finished with and everybody could sleep soundly in their bunks again.

She knew it was wrong of her to wish like that, when others had given their lives to put a stop to such goings-on; and, in particular, she thought of the poor woman who'd sacrificed herself out of love for her dead husband. But she couldn't help it . . . and, anyway, was it so very wrong to feel that Miranda and Tom Gosling and Barnacle and herself were more important than such high-sounding ideas as justice?

She glanced at Tom Gosling and saw that he too was looking at the black bag, and she wondered if his thoughts were the same as hers . . .

In part, they were. He too listened to the voices with a dull anger and fear, and he longed to be downriver again, at the Traveller's Rest, where beauty in a glass was Milly the barmaid, and the dirtiest things in his life had been horse shit and Barnacle before he'd been scrubbed.

Then he thought about the Inspector, and his anger mounted as he saw in his mind's eye that rigid, unbending man who put duty above everything and on that account had been turned into a murderer and a thief. Suddenly he felt that he understood him, almost as well as he understood himself . . .

'Why don't you tell him?' he said aloud. 'Once he knows what's been done to him, he'll move heaven and earth to bring them others to book.'

Joe and the Colonel stared at him, not pityingly, as he'd feared, but as if they were taking serious note of what he'd said.

'That's a fine idea, Mr Gosling,' said the Colonel, 'to turn their own weapon against them. But it would never do, it would never do.'

'Why do you say that, Colonel Brodsky?'

'Because, Mr Gosling, such a man, a madman for duty who has already committed such terrible acts, will struggle with all his might against the truth that he is no better than a common criminal! He will not listen. He *must* not listen. He will blot out what he hears . . . and, I fear, he will cut the throat that has dared to utter such lies! Alas, Mr Gosling, politicians know all too well the value to them of an honest man.'

'I'm sure you're right, Colonel Brodsky, and you know a deal more of the world than I do. But this Inspector, if what you've been saying about him is true, I think I know him. Although I've never, to the best of me knowledge, laid eyes on him, I think I know the sort of man he is.'

'And what sort of man is that, Mr Gosling?'

'He's a bit like some masts, Colonel Brodsky. They're very strong and straight, but sometimes, when a sudden wind catches 'em unawares, they don't bend, they don't make excuses to themselves, they break!'

He stopped and glanced quickly at Mrs McDipper to see how she was taking his interfering. She was gazing at him strangely, almost as if he was a hole in the road that hadn't been there before . . .

'My respects to you, Mr Gosling,' said Joe, quietly. 'Not that we never respected you before. I'll call back when it's getting dark and take the bag. I'll be followed by the fruit-peeling gent outside and, sooner or later, me and the Inspector will meet. And then we'll find out, Mr Gosling, when I tell him what's been done to him, whether our man bends or breaks.'

'No, Mister Joe,' said Mister Gosling. 'I'll take the bag. With respect, Mister Joe, you ain't the sort of man to do it. He wouldn't believe you, not even if you was to get down on your knees. It needs a simpler sort of man to tell him . . . a man more like himself, if you know what I mean. I think he'll believe me . . .'

Joe began to protest, but Colonel Brodsky interposed: 'Mr Gosling is right, Joseph. The truth means nothing unless you believe it.'

'But the risk – the risk, sir!'

'I think Mr Gosling understands the risk, Joseph. He is not a child. I know him better than you do, Joseph; and, although I cannot guess what is going on inside him at this moment, I know him well enough to understand him when he says that he and the Inspector are alike. Mr Gosling too has a law, a duty that he sets above everything, but his is the law of the heart, not of the State.'

'Then – be careful, sir,' muttered Joe. 'For God's sake, be careful! With a man like that you can never tell . . . It ain't worth it, sir . . . He'll use his knife . . . Be careful . . .'

'He'll kill you, Tom,' whispered Mrs McDipper hopelessly. 'He'll kill you! His knife –'

'If he don't use it on me, he'll use it on the boy, Clara.'

'The boy!' cried Mrs McDipper, her voice rising in despair. 'Oh, it was a black day when he came into our lives! He's brought us all nothing but bad luck!'

TWENTY-EIGHT

Barnacle shivered. He felt cold, right down to the bone.

'What's going on?' whispered Miranda, coming up close as he crouched beside the hatch, with his ears hanging out. 'And who's that ugly little man with the broken nose and the basket of fruit?'

'Dunno, miss,' mumbled Barnacle. 'Can't 'ear proper.'

'Liar! I saved your life, remember!'

'Yus, miss. I ain't forgot.'

Even if he'd wanted to, she wasn't going to give him the chance. She hadn't stopped reminding him since she'd woke up. But still, she had a right . . . not so much for what she'd done, but for what she hadn't done.

Although he was much obliged to her for having stopped him being knifed, he was even more obliged for something else. She'd never said a word about his having been up on the deck with the Colonel's black bag, and he respected her for having kept quiet about it. She might have saved his skin with her hook, but she saved his honour with her silence. And Barnacle had a sense of honour. It wasn't very much, and maybe you'd have had to look pretty close to have found it at all, but it was there all right, somewhere inside.

He'd certainly been meaning to help himself from the Colonel's bag, but equally certainly he would have been deeply ashamed if Mister Gosling had found out about it. He would, he felt, have been dishonoured. His sense of honour was a very particular thing. It wasn't one of them general articles what spread itself over everything, like milk; it kept with people . . .

'Eavesdroppers,' said Miranda, angry about Barnacle's ingratitude, having got no more out of him than a grunt, 'hear no good of themselves, my lad!'

Barnacle stared at her and marvelled at her female powers. She must have had ears as long as her bleeding hook, as she'd been over on the other side of the deck when her ma had said what she'd said: that it had been a black day when Barnacle had come into their lives and that he'd brought them all bad luck.

But that hadn't been the worst of it. He'd heard other things too, things that he'd only partly understood; but they'd frightened the wits out of him and sunk his spirits lower than they'd ever been before. They'd chilled him to the bone. Mrs McDipper had been dead right. Although the soot had been scrubbed off of him, he still left a black mark wherever he went. It was time he slung his hook . . .

He waited till just after six o'clock in the evening, when Mister Gosling had gone to the Jolly Bargeman to fetch back their supper, and the McDippers were below. Then he went down into the cabin. The Colonel was asleep, and the black bag was on the table. It was like it had been put out for him. He took it and fled.

'Thief! Thief!' He could hear Mister Gosling's voice inside his head just as real as if he'd actually heard it with his ears. 'Thief! Thief!'

'I ain't . . . I ain't . . .' he panted, as he stumbled along street after street, sometimes clutching the black bag to his chest and sometimes swinging it wildly and banging it into passers-by.

'Good riddance!' he could hear Mrs McDipper shouting out, and he could almost see the thankfulness on her face. 'Good riddance to bad rubbish!'

'I ain't . . . I ain't . . .' he sobbed, but the people inside his head took no notice and only pushing, shoving strangers turned to stare . . .

He had to keep away from the river and the Jolly Bargeman and all them old places. They were sure to be out looking for him . . .

'Have you seen a boy?'

'What manner of boy, Mister Gosling?'

'A boy with a bag, black as your hat!'

It was getting dark. Shops were shutting up and yellow street lamps were hiccuping and making all the doorways jump. Public houses were singing on corners about mothers and sweethearts and wives. The night had begun.

Somebody was after him. He could hear the footsteps. They was big and heavy and with a creak to them, like he was treading on birds. A big man; but he must have been wonderful quick on his feet because whenever Barnacle stopped and turned, he wasn't there. But as soon as Barnacle started up again, so did the footsteps.

He walked on. The street was thin and empty, and a single lamp-post stared into nothingness like a dead man's eye. It stood on the corner of an alley what ended up in a wall. It was a dead end.

He stopped. Not a bleeding sound. Then he began to creep down the alley –

'Brown, isn't it?' came a voice that made him shake with fright, a quiet voice with a whistle in it. 'Absalom Brown?'

He turned. Huge and black against the lamp-post's yellow gleaming stood Whistling Edge!

'I – I ain't goin' to run away, mister,' whispered Barnacle. 'Not this time.'

The Inspector began to walk towards him, and Barnacle remembered the last time Whistling Edge had come at him and held out his hand and said, 'I won't hurt you, boy.' But now he'd changed his mind. His hand was in his pocket; and Barnacle knew that when it came out there'd be a knife in it.

'Absalom Brown,' said the Inspector again, and his square, heavy face was like a stone.

'They – they calls me Barnacle, mister . . . on account of me amazin' powers of 'oldin' on.'

'To what, Barnacle?'

'To me life, mister!' screamed out Barnacle, as he saw the Inspector's hand begin to come out of his pocket. ''Ere! This is what yer after!' He fell down on his knees and held out the black bag. 'It's 'is bag! I brung it for yer, mister! 'Ere! Take it!'

The Inspector stopped. He stared at the bag, and then at the terrified Barnacle. 'So . . . you brought it for me, did you, Barnacle? Why?'

'They wanted yer to 'ave it, mister . . . They wanted to catch yer, mister . . . They wanted yer to know everyfink, mister . . .' gabbled Barnacle. And then, as fast as he could, tumbling out words on top of one another in his hurry to get them heard in time – for the Inspector's hand was slowly, slowly coming out of his pocket – he told everything!

He told about Lord Hobart and Mr Hastymite and Lord Hobart's new house in Hertfordshire and Mr Hastymite's little presents to the ladies and of how they'd been deceiving the Inspector into killing people to get them the money they wanted and they'd turned him into a common murderer and a thief. He told about Colonel Brodsky and Mister Joe and every last word they'd said; for his powers of holding on to things was still amazing, and especially now when his life depended on getting them right.

At last he came to the end of them. He stopped and gazed

up at the Inspector. He wondered if he'd done enough. Mister Gosling had said that the Inspector would break.

'These are all lies, boy,' said the Inspector at length. 'They have deceived you. They have told you lies.' His face was still like a stone.

'They never told me nuffink, mister!' pleaded Barnacle, suddenly realizing that his words had had no effect, and that he'd done the worst thing possible by coming to tell the Inspector because the Inspector could see he was a liar and a thief and didn't believe a word he'd said. 'I 'ad to listen in at the 'atch. They never told me no lies.'

'Your friends are wicked men, boy,' said the Inspector. 'The two gentlemen they accused – his lordship and Mr Hastymite – are great gentlemen. They are Ministers, boy, Ministers of State, and they are working for the good of our country. It is your friends, your Russian and your Mister Joe, who are the real enemies.'

'I dunno about countries and enemies and fings like that,' wailed Barnacle, suddenly abandoning everything and pouring out the private sorrows of his heart. 'All I knows is that I wants to 'elp my Mister Goslin' an' stop bringin' 'im bad luck! That's why I come, mister! An' then she said it were a black day when I come into their lives . . . An' 'e's losin' 'is boat . . . That's why I come, mister! I don't care nuffink about them other fings . . . 'Ere, mister! For Gawd's sake, take 'is bag!'

The Inspector tightened his lips. 'And they sent you, a child, to tell me their lies. A child!'

'They didn't send me, mister!' cried Barnacle anxiously. 'My Mister Goslin' was to 'ave come . . . but I thought you'd knife 'im, so I nicked the bag and come meself!'

'You . . . you thought I'd knife him so you came yourself?' said the Inspector slowly.

'That's right, mister. They said you was dangerous. They

said wiv a man like you it was 'ard to say what you'd do when you found out.'

'Didn't you think that I might knife you, Barnacle?'

Barnacle shrugged his shoulders hopelessly. He didn't like to say that he never thought more than an hour ahead. The Inspector was staring at him. Barnacle fancied that he was swaying slightly, as if a wind had come up.

Suddenly the Inspector spoke, and his voice was harsh. 'Your friends have been telling you lies, wicked lies. Make no mistake about it. But . . . but . . . come with me.'

He took his hand out of his pocket. He stretched it out towards Barnacle, and there was no knife in it. 'Come with me, Barnacle. I – I won't hurt you.'

'The bag, mister!' offered Barnacle uncertainly.

'Not yet . . . not yet.'

'What about this, mister?' asked Barnacle, bringing out the locket and offering it to the Inspector timidly.

The Inspector looked at it and seemed almost to shrink away.

'I thought you wanted it, mister,' persisted Barnacle, feeling that it was somehow important that the Inspector should take something from him. As he was holding the locket, it came open in his hand. The Inspector stared at the tiny picture within.

'It's – it's me ma an' me,' murmured Barnacle, from force of habit, 'when I was little . . .'

The Inspector looked at Barnacle; and for the first time, he smiled. 'Maybe so . . . maybe so. Come with me.'

TWENTY-NINE

Just before midnight, two figures stood outside a house in a fashionable square off Pall Mall, in a manner that could only be described as loitering, though it was hard to say with what intent. One was a big, square-built man, dressed like a respectable tradesman, and the other was a skinny runt of a boy carrying a black bag. All the windows of the house were lit, and sounds of celebration were drifting down into the square; and the two loiterers were staring up at it as if they'd never seen a house before. A queer pair; and the policeman on his beat paused to have a word.

'Nothin' unpleasant in mind, I hope?' he inquired, with a warning look towards the houses under his care. 'Nothin' that you wouldn't want your mother to know about, eh?'

'I hope not,' said the Inspector, and the policeman walked on. 'The locket. Give me the locket, boy.' This was the first time the Inspector had spoken to Barnacle. They had walked all the way, side by side, without a single word having passed between them. Barnacle gave him the locket. He didn't wish him luck. He didn't think the Inspector wanted it. He held out the bag. The Inspector shook his head.

'Keep it till I come out again,' he said. Then, for a second time, he smiled. 'You trusted me, Barnacle, so now I must trust you.'

He left the boy and began to mount the steps to the front door. He paused and glanced back. Barnacle was standing stock-still and staring up at the top of the house.

'What are you looking at?' he called out softly.

'Chimneys, mister. I should never 'ave fallen down . . . not wiv me amazin' powers of 'oldin' on.'

The house was full of guests. It was Lord Hobart's birthday, and everyone wished him well. Even quite humble people, who didn't know him, had sent him touching little presents, for he was the spirit of Old England and was loved and respected throughout the land. He was in a rollicking, rolling, cigar-puffing mood, something between bluff King Hal and old King Cole; and he was none too pleased when he was told that Inspector Creaker was waiting to see him urgently. It was, after all, his birthday.

'Well, Inshpector,' he said, coming into the quiet little panelled room on the right of the hall where his lordship conducted his private business, 'what is it? I'm afraid you have come at an – an inconvenient time. A li'l celebration. My – ha ha! – birthday!'

He travelled carefully across the floor towards the fireplace and leaned against it, mountainous and smoking and looking for somewhere steady on which to rest his glass of wine.

'My congratulations, m'lord,' said Inspector Creaker, 'but it is a matter of some importance.'

'Yes, yes!' grunted his lordship, very much occupied with the rival claims of his wine glass and his cigar. 'So . . . so I understand. But please be quick about it. I have guests, y'know. So what is it, man? Come out with it – come out with it!'

'It is this, m'lord.'

'What, what? What the devil have you got there? Come over here, man. You don't expect me to come to you?' said

Lord Hobart, peering irritably at the Inspector, who was holding something in his hand.

Obediently the Inspector approached the great man. His lordship looked carefully. The man was holding out the locket. *The locket!* Suddenly Lord Hobart beamed, and in a twinkling, his face expressed all the warmth and open-heartedness that had endeared him to millions!

'So . . . so . . .,' he cried, 'you've got it! Shplendid, shplendid! I knew you'd succeed! My dear fellow, my dear fellow! And the funds? You've laid hands on them, of course?' He drank off his wine, and puffed fiercely at his cigar, and searched for the Inspector through the smoke.

'The boy, m'lord,' said the Inspector.

'The – the boy?' inquired Lord Hobart, momentarily at a loss to understand what the Inspector was talking about. 'Oh yes, that boy. Very unfortunate business. But all in the course of duty, eh, Inspector? Where our country is concerned, we must all make sacrifices. You have . . . er . . . put a stop to his birthdays? After all, we – we can't all have them, eh, eh?'

'The boy has told me certain things, m'lord,' said the Inspector, unmoved by his lordship's expressions of sympathy.

'Told you? Told you what?' began Lord Hobart, when the door opened and Mr Hastymite came in. He too was a little flushed with wine, but he did not seem to find the floor as treacherous as did Lord Hobart.

He shut the door and, smiling courteously, said: 'Ah! I heard that our good friend had called.'

'Hastymite!' cried his lordship, waving his cigar in the air and scattering ash. 'He has the funds, thank God!'

'Is that so, Inspector?' inquired Mr Hastymite keenly.

The Inspector ignored him. He continued to address himself to Lord Hobart. 'The boy,' he repeated, 'has told me certain things. He told me that he heard that you and Mr Hastymite – '

'Eh? Eh?' interrupted his lordship, beginning to raise his

voice, as he felt that the Inspector's manners left something to be desired. 'He heard what? Out with it, man!'

'He told me that he heard that you have been keeping the funds I have brought you for your own private purposes, m'lord. He heard –'

Lord Hobart's waving cigar jerked and collided with the wine glass on the mantelpiece. It fell and smashed.

'Damn him!' shouted Lord Hobart, before Mr Hastymite could stop him. 'Damn him, damn him! I told you, Hastymite! I warned you that that little animal up the chimney had heard us!'

'Be quiet, man!' muttered Mr Hastymite, very white in the face. 'You –'

He stopped. There had been a knock on the door, followed by the appearance of the splendid Lady Hobart. She looked round the room. 'Oh! I see you are busy,' she said, with a vague air of annoyance. 'Try not to be too long. The guests, you know. A very unsuitable time, Inspector . . .'

The door closed behind her, and there was silence. Mr Hastymite looked from the enraged and alarmed Lord Hobart to the stony-faced Inspector. With a man like that, he thought, there was nothing further to be gained by evasion. It would be better to be open . . .

'Well,' he said quietly, 'it seems as if the Inspector has been doing some inspecting. But surely, my dear Inspector –'

'Creaker!' broke in the mountainous politician, biting his cigar to shreds with agitation. 'You are not to say anything about this! I forbid it! Do you understand?'

'Yes, m'lord,' said the Inspector. 'I believe I do.'

'Then if you value your post,' went on Lord Hobart, summoning up all the threatening power that had crushed many a political opponent, 'hold your tongue! These matters are not to be discussed outside this room! I demand loyalty, loyalty!'

'Come, come, my lord!' said Mr Hastymite quickly. 'The Inspector is a very loyal person. We have always known that. And now . . . well, he is one of us. Isn't that so, Inspector?'

'If you say so, sir,' said the Inspector, remotely.

'A – a glass of brandy, Inspector?' urged Mr Hastymite, glancing at Lord Hobart and hoping that his lordship would have the good sense not to antagonize the man. The Inspector was, Mr Hastymite sensed, very delicately balanced, and with a man like him you could never tell . . .

The Inspector shook his head. He was, thought Mr Hastymite, taking it very calmly. Certainly he was showing no sign of turning against them.

'No? Well, I imagine you are looking for something a little more substantial, Inspector. Very well. I think you can rely on us to – to reward you for your – er – efforts, your splendid efforts, Inspector.'

'So he wants a share, eh?' said Lord Hobart, suddenly jerking into life and scowling at his ruined cigar. 'He wants a share!'

'As you see, my dear Inspector,' said Mr Hastymite with a strained little laugh, 'his lordship believes in plain speaking! After all, he's famous for it!'

'So that's why he didn't bring the funds with him,' said Lord Hobart, his voice heavy with contempt. 'Where are they, Creaker? Or d'you mean to keep it all for yourself, eh, eh?'

'I'm sure the Inspector had no such thoughts, my lord!' said Mr Hastymite anxiously. 'I think it would be better if we discussed the matter sensibly . . . a little later. Perhaps we have had a little too much wine . . . A little later, when we are all calm . . . eh, Inspector? Inspector!'

Mr Hastymite had to raise his voice, as the Inspector seemed to have fallen into a reverie. But he had apparently heard what had been suggested.

'Tonight,' he said abruptly. 'At Blackfriars Stairs. I will have the bag – the funds – ready for you.'

'At what time, Inspector?'

The Inspector frowned, and then took out a watch. It was Colonel Brodsky's.

'Ah!' said Lord Hobart, observing the enamelled black eagle. 'I see he has already helped himself . . . our loyal, honest man!'

'At four o'clock,' said the Inspector, putting away the watch. Mr Hastymite was much relieved that the man hadn't flared up at Lord Hobart's accusation.

'Four o'clock?' repeated Lord Hobart, lighting a fresh cigar and enveloping himself in smoke. 'What a God-forsaken hour, man!'

'As you say, m'lord,' agreed the Inspector. 'God-forsaken.'

THIRTY

The policeman in the square observed the big man go inside the house and leave the boy waiting on the pavement outside. He made a note of it, and continued on his beat. Some twenty minutes later, when he returned, he observed that the boy was still there. He didn't appear to have moved so much as an eyeball. Shortly after, the big man came out of the house and, taking hold of the boy roughly by the shoulder, hurried him away so fast as almost to drag him off his feet.

It was, thought the policeman, who was a reflective individual and liked to ponder deeply on the mysteries of the night, a rum go. He made a note of it.

The Inspector dragged Barnacle along as far as the Strand. Then he stopped. Barnacle looked up at him.

'Well, mister?'

The Inspector didn't answer. He seemed lost in thought. Suddenly he put his hand in his pocket. Barnacle flinched; but it was only the locket. Silently he gave it to Barnacle.

'Did it – did it bring yer luck, mister?'

The Inspector stared at him. 'Give me the bag, boy,' he said. Barnacle gave it to him. 'Do you know where you are, boy?' Barnacle nodded. 'Then go now! Go back to your – your Mister Gosling! Tell him – tell him not to leave his moorings tonight. Do you understand that? No matter what cause, what tide, what business he has! He must not go on the river tonight! Now, go!'

'But, mister –'

'I told you to go, Barnacle!' suddenly shouted the Inspector, his eyes blazing with anger. 'And when Inspector Creaker tells a boy to go, he runs! Run, boy, run, run, run, *run*!'

His voice rose almost to a scream, and Barnacle, with a last look of terror and bewilderment, fled.

For a few moments the Inspector stared after the frightened, scuttling child, and then, when he'd vanished down one of the streets that led down to the river, he began to walk and walk through the dark town.

He walked swiftly, carrying the black bag, with his heavy, caped overcoat swinging and flapping like the damaged wings of some huge bird. Night people, the homeless, the lost, the shadowy drifters and the glaring drunkards who saw horrors in lamp-posts and demons in pillarboxes, stared after him. Constable Rook saw him near Fleet Street, saluted and wished him goodnight, but he might as well have spoke to a runaway horse for all the answer he got. He was after somebody, the constable concluded; and God help them when they was caught. The look on the Inspector's face had been enough to turn a man to stone.

The Inspector was a haunted man. At every turn, in every dark alley and every dingy courtyard, he saw a ghost. It was the ghost of the woman he'd killed. She watched him from windows, she stared out at him from doorways, and always with the same look on her face: fear and hate.

It was a look that had always troubled him and lingered obstinately in his mind. Although such a look had long been familiar to him in the course of his work, hers, he felt, had been something more. Now he knew what it had been. She had stared back at him not only with fear and hatred but also with loathing, disgust and contempt.

She had known him better than he'd known himself. He was a common murderer and a thief. His world was in ruins, and the staff that had always supported him, duty, had turned, like Aaron's rod, into a writhing, poisonous snake.

He was in Farringdon Street. His pace slowed down. He was near his destination. He turned into Clerkenwell Road and from there made his way among the little lanes and alleys off Clerkenwell Green, where the clockmakers and manufacturers of mechanical marvels lived. At length he stopped outside a dingy little shop above which was inscribed, in gilt lettering so worn and faded that it could scarcely be read: 'H. Todd. Maker of Clocks and Toys'.

The Inspector knocked on the door. After a few moments, a light glimmered and a hoarse voice demanded to know who was there. For answer, the Inspector knocked again. The door opened and the nightgowned maker of clocks and toys, holding up an ingenious lantern (very suitable as a birthday gift for boys), peered out. As soon as he saw who his caller was, he went pale with alarm and the lantern began to shake.

'W-what do you want, Mr Inspector, sir?'

'A favour, Mr Todd.'

'At this time of night, Mr Inspector, sir? What is it?'

'Something from your back room, Mr Todd. One of your particular toys.'

The maker of clocks and toys fiddled with his lantern, and a beam shot out of it like magic and illuminated the Inspector's face. Mr Todd peered inquisitively into his caller's eyes. Then he nodded; 'Come inside, Mr Inspector, sir, come inside . . .'

Lord Hobart and Mr Hastymite sat side by side in a hackney cab as they were rattled and jolted along towards Blackfriars Stairs. They were in evening dress, and the fitful glow of Lord Hobart's cigar made their diamond studs glitter like sparks in a fire.

'Why the devil couldn't he have brought it to the house?'

muttered his lordship. 'This is madness, Hastymite, madness!'

'He was in no mood to argue,' murmured Mr Hastymite, thankful that the worst effects of the wine had worn off the great man, and he was not likely to make any more blunders.

'Mood? Who the devil cares about his mood?'

'One must be careful with a man like him, my lord. Remember, he hasn't had our advantages –'

'What? Do you mean he hasn't been to a decent school?'

'Among other things, my lord. I think it is quite understandable that a man like him, the son of God knows who, would find himself at a disadvantage in your house. He wants our little talk to be among equals. It's his way of bringing us down to his level, my lord.'

'The scoundrel! The damned scoundrel! But – but do you think we can trust him?'

'Oh, I think so, my lord. He's too deeply in himself. After all, his was the hand that – that – um – performed its duty.'

His lordship shrugged his huge shoulders and puffed fiercely at his cigar until the inside of the cab glowed like a furnace. At last the cab halted and the driver peered down through the hatch. ''Ere we are, gentlemen. Blackfriars. Do you want me to wait?'

Idly he wondered what cheerful devilry, what elderly mischief, two such gentlemen could be up to in such a place at such a time of night.

'We may be some little time, cabby,' said Mr Hastymite, getting out and paying the fare and then assisting his great companion to the ground.

'That's all right, sir,' said the cabby. 'I ain't likely to pick up another fare at four o'clock in the morning.'

The river was foggy, and the lamps along the embankment floated weirdly in the thick and rolling air.

'Ah! There he is!' exclaimed Mr Hastymite. 'Our good and faithful Inspector!'

'I'll wait for you 'ere, sir,' said the cabby, as the two gentlemen, in silk-lined capes and jaunty silk hats, walked together towards an indistinct figure who waited under a distant lamp.

'I – I don't like it, Hastymite,' muttered his lordship.

'No more do I, my lord. But we must all make sacrifices for those little extra things in life that we want!'

As they approached, the Inspector came forward and saluted them courteously. Lord Hobart stared at him suspiciously.

'Where are the funds, man? I don't see any bag.'

'Down there, m'lord,' said the Inspector, pointing to the stone steps that led down into the river. 'In my boat.'

'Well, fetch it, man.'

The Inspector hesitated. He looked about him; he glanced towards the waiting cab. 'I would prefer you to come down, m'lord,' he said quietly. 'There are people about . . . I have a man who passes here . . . and your cabby, m'lord . . . It is better that we should be private . . . in my boat.'

He began to descend the stairs, beckoning to the two gentlemen to follow. They peered down into the darkness. They could see the boat, heaving and sighing gently against the steps. The Inspector was already seated in it, and at his feet was a substantial black bag with a silver clasp. Again the Inspector beckoned.

'Be careful, m'lord,' he called out softly. 'And you, Mr Hastymite. The steps are slippery.'

They went aboard, and the Inspector's boat, although it was sturdy, tipped and tilted alarmingly under Lord Hobart's tremendous weight.

'Not exactly the ship of State, Hastymite,' he grunted as he settled himself down, and then, adjusting himself to the gentle rocking and feeling the nearness of the water, he put his hand over the side and said: 'D'you know, this is the first time that I've been in a rowing-boat since I was a child?' He chuckled; and then his eyes fixed themselves on the black bag.

'We'll row out a little way,' said the Inspector, pushing off from the side. 'It's best not to be seen. Only a little way, m'lord, a few yards.'

The oars splashed and streaked the water with silver, and the stone steps dissolved into the fog. The Inspector rowed easily. His face was calm and mild. Presently he shipped his oars and the boat drifted in nothingness. He lifted up the bag, and gently, as if it was as tender as a baby, he passed it to Lord Hobart.

'The funds, m'lord.'

'I take it,' said his lordship, 'that you already know what is in it?'

'Yes, m'lord.'

'Then what's your price? How much of it do you want?'

'I think,' breathed the Inspector, watching the bag intently, 'that you will find that there is more than enough for all of us in the bag.'

'We'll be the judge of that, my good man,' grunted his lordship, and began to fumble with the clasp. 'It's very stiff, Hastymite,' he complained. 'Here! You try.'

Mr Hastymite took the bag. His fingers were more supple than his lordship's. 'Ah!' he exclaimed as the clasp unfastened, and he looked up in triumph.

There was a faint click and Mr Hastymite just had time to see the strangest expression on the Inspector's face. It was a look of wild joy!

As the Inspector had foretold, there was more than enough for all of them in the black bag. The maker of clocks and toys had done his work well.

The cabby, who was patiently waiting for his gentlemen, saw a red rose begin to bloom in the fog over the river. Then it turned yellow, and then glaring white. It was accompanied by a huge explosion that shook the cab and made the horse rear and scream. Then fragments of wood began to patter down on to the embankment and even on to the roof of the cab. Among them, to the cabby's horror and disgust, was a gentleman's hand, still wearing its white glove.

'Bombs,' said the cabby, when over and over again he told his friends, 'do queer things.'

But queerer even than the cabby's adventure was a happening on the river itself. When the turmoil of the explosion had subsided, another disturbance arose. Deep under the water, a shadowy shape began to move and drift and turn, and a moon-white face, with slowly dancing black hair, began to rise up and up and up . . .

It was the murdered woman. The violence of the explosion had freed her body and brought it to the surface. At last the Inspector's crime had come out of its darkness.

THIRTY-ONE

'Donia Vassilova'. The name was inscribed on a plain wooden cross, which was the best that could be obtained in so short a time. She had been buried in a small, sunshiny City churchyard, a haunt of starlings and sparrows, with tall iron railings to keep the Dearly Remembereds in and dogs and children out.

Considering the haste of the arrangements, the burial service had gone off very creditably, and the turn-out of mourners, thought the parson, was nothing of which the lady herself might have felt ashamed – at least, apart from the wretched little boy who had attended in check trousers and a bright yellow waistcoat with vulgar buttons the size of half-crowns. The only indication of bereavement about him was a thin black ribbon tied round his arm.

Barnacle himself felt it keenly. Everybody else was in black: Lord Mounteagle, Mister Joe, old Colonel Brodsky, leaning on his stick and with his beard as black as a boot, and Mister Gosling and the McDippers. There was even a bleeding cat watching the birds what was in mourning . . . most likely in advance of what it was aiming to do. It was only he, Barnacle, what had nothing better than a ribbon. He'd been a sight more respectful before he'd been scrubbed. *Then* he'd been black all over.

'A very brave woman,' murmured Lord Mounteagle, gazing down on the quiet earth, and Mrs McDipper sobbed gently into her handkerchief for the woman who had died for love.

'She is at peace,' said Colonel Brodsky, wincing and being supported by Joe. 'A sort of justice has been done.'

'Justice?' wondered Lord Mounteagle. 'I wish I knew what it was! Sometimes I think I am no wiser now than when I was a child and wept and cried that something wasn't fair.'

'Ah! He hasn't changed, Joseph, even after all these years,' sighed the Colonel. 'Still seeking wisdom in the heart of a child.'

'I fancy there's worse places you could look,' said Joe. 'Such as down a coal hole or in the Houses of Parliament. Rest your weight on me, sir.'

'Thank you, thank you! Tell me, Joseph, how do I look now? Be honest, Joseph.'

Joe looked at him carefully. 'All things considered, sir, I'd say you looked a good ten years younger!'

'Only ten, Joseph? Ah! I was hoping for twenty!'

The little group of mourners began to move away from the graveside – all except Barnacle, who lingered. He still felt badly about his lack of outward grief. Somehow it didn't seem right because he *did* feel sad. It wasn't only for her, the woman, who he'd never known; it was for him too, for old Whistling Edge, the Inspector who'd done her in. He couldn't help it, but he wept in his heart for that strange, stern man who had smiled at him twice and told him to run.

He took out the locket and put it down on the grave.

'You can't leave it there, lad,' said Mister Gosling, coming back to investigate Barnacle's curious activities.

'It weren't never mine, mister,' said Barnacle sadly. 'Not reely. It belonged to 'er, I s'pose. 'E'd 'ave wanted 'er to 'ave it back.'

Mister Gosling looked at him oddly. Then he knelt down,

picked up the locket and hastened with it after Lord Mounteagle. His lordship waited, and Mister Gosling asked with all respect, if, in view of Barnacle's outstanding contribution to the well-being of the world in general, his lad might be allowed to keep the locket for himself.

'He sets great store by it, your lordship.'

Lord Mounteagle pondered the matter. He inquired of Colonel Brodsky whether he had any objection. Colonel Brodsky gravely replied that he had none. He asked Joe. Joe scratched his head, brushed some earth off his master's coat and said it was no skin off his nose. Then Mrs McDipper and Miranda were applied to. They shook their heads.

'Very well, Mr Gosling,' said his lordship. 'All the world seems agreed that the boy should keep the locket. But see he takes care of it. It is quite valuable.'

'D'you fink,' asked Barnacle, clutching the locket and hope rising within him, 'I'd get 'leven pound for it?'

'Eleven pounds?' Lord Mounteagle frowned. 'Hm. Show me.'

Barnacle handed over the locket. Lord Mounteagle examined it. Barnacle prayed. Then Lord Mounteagle passed the locket to Joe. 'What do you think, Joe?'

Joe studied it and Barnacle cursed himself for suggesting too much. 'Well, it's gold all right,' said Joe. 'And the stones are diamonds. I'd say,' – Barnacle's heart stopped – 'I'd say more like a hundred and eleven. In fact, I'd go so far as to say it would be cheap at a hundred and twenty.'

Barnacle's heart danced. Sunshine exploded within him and angels sang in his ears, and their song was: *'A hundred and twenty pounds!'*

'Listen to me, Barnacle,' said Lord Mounteagle seriously. 'I've a fancy for that locket myself. I would like it to remind me of a very brave woman . . . and – and of a boy for much the same reason. I won't cheat you. I will give you, say, a hundred and fifty pounds. D'you think that would be fair, Joe?'

'Two hundred would be fairer,' said Joe, finding more earth to brush off his master.

'Thank you very much, Joe,' said Lord Mounteagle. 'I could have got it for a hundred and fifty.'

In due proportion to Barnacle's size, learning, social position and importance to the Nation, two hundred pounds in golden sovereigns was roughly equal to a kingdom of the larger sort. He walked on air, and his gestures were the gestures of a king. Had he not been so rich, he would have been insufferable.

He visited Mister Levy's shop. Right away. He insisted upon it . . .

'Why, Mrs McDipper!' cried Mister Levy, as customers came into his shop. 'What an honour! I was only saying to Mrs Levy this morning that –'

'Here's your customer, Mister Levy,' interrupted Mrs McDipper, and pointed.

'The young gentleman!' exclaimed Mister Levy, beholding Barnacle with unbounded admiration. 'So smart he looks! Savile Row, perhaps? What can I do for you today, young man? Another weskit?'

Barnacle looked at him loftily. 'That there Wappin' rat you 'ad, mister.'

'He means,' explained Mrs McDipper, with something between a frown and a smile, 'what you were pleased to call your Russian sable cape, Mister Levy. I think.'

'Ah! The sables, the sables!' Mister Levy rushed and bustled to produce the gorgeous article from which a moth arose with a melancholy, homeless air. 'Beautiful, beautiful! And – and gentlemen are wearing them today! Go down Bond Street and you'd be surprised!'

‘’Ow much?’ asked Barnacle, unmoved by what was going on in Bond Street.

‘Well, if I was to say a pound, I’d be robbing myself.’

‘Done,’ said Barnacle. ‘Give it to ’er.’ He pointed to Miranda.

‘He can afford it, Mister Levy,’ assured Mrs McDipper.

Mister Levy beamed happily and presented the cape to Miranda, who instantly burst into tears.

‘It’s all right, miss,’ said Barnacle kindly. ‘It’s only for savin’ me life. But I ain’t done yet.’

‘A pair of trousers?’ suggested Mister Levy.

‘That,’ said Barnacle, pointing to the stately remains of Captain McDipper. ‘Give yer ’leven pound.’

‘Barnacle!’ burst out Mister Gosling, who felt he could no longer leave matters to Mrs McDipper, as he generally did in Mister Levy’s shop. ‘What are you thinking of, lad?’

‘What do you want it for, Barnacle?’ asked Mrs McDipper, unaccountably blushing with confusion. She thought she knew . . .

‘They’re – they’re wearing them –’ began Mister Levy helplessly.

‘It’s for ’im,’ said Barnacle. ‘It’s for my Mister Goslin’.’

Mister Gosling turned away, and even Mrs McDipper tried to hide her face. ‘Oh, Barnacle, Barnacle!’ she cried. ‘Don’t waste your money on them old things! They’d – they’d never fit! Your Mister Gosling, my dear, is a much bigger man than ever Captain McDipper was!’

They walked back to Broken Wharf, Mister Gosling and Barnacle together and Mrs McDipper and her daughter some little way behind. As they walked, Barnacle was a little downcast that Mister Gosling was not splendid in blue and gold, but was much the same as he’d always been. Then Barnacle remembered the first time they’d walked together towards Broken Wharf, and reflected that Mister Gosling had improved upon acquaintance to a wonderful extent. He hoped, but with no great certainty, that he'd done so himself.

''Ow much,' he asked timidly, 'would it cost to buy the *Lady*, mister?'

Mister Gosling thought. 'About a hundred and twenty pounds, lad.'

'Good,' said Barnacle. 'Then we got enough.'

For a moment, he thought Mister Gosling was going to deny him, but the big man nodded and smiled. They said no more to each other after that; there weren't no need. They went down the steps to the wharf like they was floating, and they walked over the cobbles like they wasn't there. Then they went aboard the *Lady* and waited for her with the frying pan and her with the hook.

They came across the cobbles still in mourning: Mrs McDipper like a big black chrysanthemum and her girl in her Wapping sables, very stately and grand. They was more like a sweep's birthday than ashes to ashes and dust to dust; the air was full of the smell of carnations, enough to knock you flat.

'We're men of property, miss,' said Barnacle to Miranda. 'My Mister Goslin' an' me.'

He beamed. He couldn't help it. The climbing boy had reached the top. He was right up in the sky.